Thoughts from readers of *Fireworks!*, the author's first book:

My husband isn't much of a reader, but he really liked it and said that you and he are on the same page on many things.

I am enjoying your book and feel like you are in the same room talking. I do find myself laughing, snickering and identifying with so much of what you say.

I'm not much of a reader, mostly just the Bible, yet I found myself longing to grab ahold to see your solutions to our problems time and time again. It's been to the beach, pool and plane.

Finished your book and really enjoyed it. You do such a good job of putting into words what I think but can't express. I've recommended it to several of my friends and my children.

I'm still in Kauai and just finished your book. Great job, many good laughs and can't wait to see if Noxzema really works. You brought me into every chapter as if I was sitting with you and you were speaking only to me. Can't wait for your next one.

Old Lady Porn

Short Stories to Take to Bed at Night

By

Leslie Baker

www.bookstandpublishing.com

Published by
Bookstand Publishing
Morgan Hill, CA 95037
4798_4

Copyright © 2020 by Leslie Baker
All rights reserved. No part of this publication may be reproduced or transmitted in any form or by any means, electronic or mechanical, including photocopy, recording, or any information storage and retrieval system, without permission in writing from the copyright owner.

ISBN 978-1-63498-964-0

Photo by Alex Harvey on Unsplash
Cover Design by Leslie Baker

Disclaimer

This is a work of fiction. Any resemblance of the characters herein to actual persons, living or dead, is entirely coincidental.

Introduction

Porn? As in *pornography?* Porn for old ladies?! Is that what this trash is?

Well, yes and no. As we *become* old ladies, what satisfies us as 'porn' may evolve. A hot young stud dancing for dollars tucked into his thong may have been a turn-on 40 or more years ago but it seems a little declasse at this stage. Now, we're likely to find a box of Godivas or bottle of good red wine more titillating. Sad, but true.

The writer's groups I belong to are disproportionately populated with old ladies, which has me speculating that writing has become a stimulating activity for many of us. There's just the teensiest bit of imagination applied to the included stories about those groups, but you might join one and find that *writing* about your fantasies is a passable substitute for the real thing.

Another sub-section which is definitely *not* comprised of porn are the Yesterday's News stories scattered throughout. I write a column which appears in our local paper a couple of times a month and most of them are more political than anyone would want to see here. These are more personal or whimsical and shouldn't offend anyone brave enough to tackle *porn*!

Aunt Bertha is a cantankerous old broad who insisted on putting in her two-cents worth. As a mutual friend said of her: "Her forte is think pieces; she lays out the issue, states her viewpoint and leaves it to the reader to gin up his own beliefs. I like that." Bertha's stuff and mine are similar, but she doesn't have the restrictions imposed by a newspaper column.

As you read these little ditties, you may think you recognize your neighbor or sister-in-law. But, no, I've not been eavesdropping or spying, our stories are just a lot more universal than we tend to think and that can actually be kind of comforting.

You're not going to find anything too hardcore in here, but you will find a few things to tickle your fancy. And, if all you're trying to do is relax into a good night's sleep (which has sure become an unrequited dream for many of us) here is a collection of very short tales that might bring a tear to your eye, put a smile on your face or revive some memories as you snuggle under.

The Decision

When the day finally came to leave him she couldn't resist, even as frazzled as she was, a little parting shot.

It had been a wrenching decision not made easier by the length of time taken to reach it. They had two small children, *she* had a nowhere job which wouldn't support three of them and she was humiliated as hell to have to admit that her family had been right about her sorry excuse for a husband. Yes, she knew Mom and Dad would take the kids and her in for as long as it took, but this was a nasty tasting old crow, anyway.

The man was a grunting pig. Right from the get-go, he'd lumbered through her life like a jailer. When he wasn't off on one of his three-day benders, which included hundreds of miles, whores and dollars, he'd been lousy company and a worse father. She had no idea how he kept his job, but the fact that he was a good provider may be what had kept *her* imprisoned for so long. The main job qualification for the position Grunt held was a willingness to spend 6 hours a day sixty miles from anywhere and 2 hours a day in a company van getting there and back. About enough time to sleep off a hangover.

Her job was really only for pocket money and had no growth opportunities. She spent most of her paycheck on childcare, so future endeavors were going to have to be a lot more focused on income. Rationalizing staying with Grunt by saying the kids needed a father was really just her saying she was scared to death about her financial situation.

The kids were so little that, if she got them out of here quickly enough, they might forget all about him. Even if he was paying child-support and had technical visitation rights, it would only take one or two visits from Child Welfare to determine he wasn't anyone's idea of father material. He wouldn't even *want* to see them except for the impact it would have on her. He would want to hurt her in any way possible and if it meant hurting the kids, too, that certainly wasn't out of the realm of possibility.

Luckily, her folks lived several states away and Grunt knew that her Dad was perfectly capable of (and willing to) blow the old 12-gauge right through the middle of his sorry ass. Which would solve a lot of *her* problems, but she wouldn't hold her breath.

OLD LADY PORN

One of her myriad morning chores was to pack a mammoth lunch for Grunt to take that sixty miles to work every day. He might stride into the kitchen the evening before to tell her how lousy the last ham had been or how he hated the current brand of potato chips. His berating of her was about the only interaction the couple had anymore. His two daily sandwiches were huge and comprised the only food he'd see out in the middle of nowhere between their silent breakfast and dinner times.

She planned her escape for the Friday before a coming three-day weekend. Grunt was going to leave directly from work that day and head to his buddy's house in the next state over for another debauched weekend.

Things usually concealed by drawers had been carefully packed into the trunk of her car leaving only the most obvious necessities for her to grab and pack as she and the kids sprinted on their escape after he left home Friday morning. After weeks of squirreling away most of their savings, she got the last of the checking account money at the drive-thru on the way out of town. Luckily, all of Grunt's spending was with the credit card, so for three days, nothing would alert him to the empty bank accounts.

Miles down the road, with the babies securely buckled in, the wind in her hair and a smile creeping across her face, she glanced at the dashboard clock and realized that he was just about now biting into the first of his sandwiches. Both of which were layered with so much salt that she'd emptied the round, blue box on them. Hasta la vista, baby.

A Tidbit

What a pain in the ass flying is these days. Even when you can afford the relative comfort of first class, there's nothing enjoyable in the process.

She'd have been happier to get the firm to spring for XO or some other charter outfit, but so far, first class was as good as it got. As she settled in, made sure that her laptop was accessible and accepted the first glass of champagne she could get her hands on, she quickly surveyed the other passengers. The usual. People studiously ignoring each other while they busied themselves with *looking* busy. She hadn't made more than the most cursory eye contact with the guy to her left when she sat down and didn't plan to further that.

After shooting back one more glass of Krug, she leaned her head back and reluctantly began to contemplate how she was going to negotiate the contract lurking in that flat case at her side.

Leslie Baker

"I saw you take inventory of our fellow sardines," came a voice from her left, "do you take this flight often?" Uh, no, she reluctantly answered while not opening her eyes. The undeterred fellow rattled on a bit about not recognizing her on this route he apparently plied frequently.

Still without turning her head, opening her eyes or elaborating, she told him that she usually flew into Boston.

"Ah. And are you a member?" he asked.

Slowly and deliberately she raised and turned her head to see intense brown eyes looking directly at her. "Well, for you, yes, I believe I am;" she replied as she took his measure. Since hers was the aisle seat, she left first for a meeting of that most exclusive of societies: The Anonymous Mile High Club.

OLD LADY PORN

May and December

Tendrils of the coffee's aroma drifted to him as he began to wake. Only a few years ago, he'd often heard the pot downstairs as it started to brew at 4:30, signaling the start of his day. But, like so much else, he doesn't hear it these days.

His wife, still asleep beside him, has mentioned in other contexts that the sense of smell is among the last of the five to go. He smiles as he reflects on the varied knowledge they've brought to this relationship.

Theirs is a May/December pairing which has worked for twenty years. For so long, her relative youth inspired him to keep up both physically and mentally. He's much more adept at the technology required just to make a damned phone call than are many friends his own age. She's dragged him along even when he didn't think he had it in him. Without wanting to be his best for her, he probably wouldn't still be in the gym several days a week.

He's been a calming presence and level head when she threatened to go off the rails over the years; older and wiser in many ways. They've balanced out pretty well.

She's no longer the fifty-year-old babe she was when they met. She's thickened around the middle, droops where she didn't and has begun to show her 70 years. He hadn't actually seen her naked for a while when he recently ran into her in the laundry room stripping off her nightgown for the already running load in the washer. 'Why, you're an old woman!' he'd blurted in shock. He still feels bad about that, he could see in her eyes that it wounded.

But then, he's not the stud he once was, either. The gym can do only so much to stave off the years. And sex is a distant memory. As a recent widower of 70 when they met, he'd been as randy as a teenager with no censorious parents around to curb his activities. With a still full head of hair and the body of the athlete he'd always been, no one ever believed his age. Now, at ninety, it's easier to convince them of it. Today she is the same age he was when they met; seventy and still needing to be active while he is content spending many days reclining in front of the television.

This is a hard time of transition for them both. They've always done many things together and complimented each other so well that it's hard to adapt to drastically different energy levels and needs for social interaction. Over the last ten years or so, he's scaled way back on the work he puts into maintaining their small business. It still bothers him to see her over there for long hours doing what she loves to do and, while he realizes that it's not fair to expect her to radically alter *her* activity just because he has, he hasn't found a way to be comfortable with it. He helps with the laundry and some of the chores that used to be her purview, but there's no way to not feel the new imbalances in their relationship.

Beyond the physical adjustments in their marriage, he's aware of emotional separations setting in. He can feel her watching him for changes in his health and it's hard to not resent being monitored. He realizes that it's part of her make-up to recognize and respond to signs of aging and decline; but, truthfully, he doesn't like talking about his exhaustion and sleepless nights. She must look at each new 'symptom' as yet another shortening of their relationship and in her life as she knows it. Yes, as she's said, she could get hit by a bus tomorrow and leave *him* as the widower, but you kind of have to go with the odds and see her as the one in black.

In his mind, he doesn't *feel* like an old guy on the decline. It isn't how he views himself. Not until he has trouble with the stairs, gets confused or can't move his bowels. In his *head*, he's still vital and truckin' on.

She feels totally confused about who she is and how to approach her life these days and it's making her grouchy. For so long she'd kept him younger than his years but now it feels like he's making her older than hers. She's floundering. In the past, they'd come very close to splitting the sheets a few times, but have persevered and to leave him now, when he's become an old man, isn't an option. She said 'for better or for worse' and meant it.

Her conundrum is: how do you suddenly learn to help an older person to navigate the end years of his life while maintaining some sort of age-appropriate life for yourself? She has a friend whose husband suffered a stroke that has put them in a very similar situation. Both of these men could live many years more; they're not on life support or unable to enjoy the occasional good time, but they are struggling with more and more aspects of everyday life. The women are endeavoring to enrich their husbands' quality of life while having a life themselves.

The husband is aware of his wife's irritation, certainly, but doesn't connect it directly to himself. He feels that she's just going to be one of those old people who get grumpy. He doesn't see how hard she tries to be content with television rather than conversation and friends. And she hasn't yet learned how to take up hobbies and activities that don't include him.

OLD LADY PORN

Since this became their new normal, she's wryly remembered her elderly mother having counseled her to not marry a man so much older. But like so much of mom's advice, it went unheeded.

She's not interested in another marriage if she should outlive him. She's heard from too many friends who, upon dipping a toe into the dating pool after being widowed, affirmed the old adage that, at this stage of life, most men just want a purse or a nurse. Most women are burned out on nurse duty by then and, if they have that much of a purse, they can go out to play with a bunch of other merry widows.

The couple's purse won't stretch too far if long term care is needed or if they have to opt for a senior living facility, so staying in their home is more of a necessity than a choice even if it's one they've made willingly.

In these situations, there's not much comfort for anyone in knowing that it's playing out in countless homes all over the world.

Leslie Baker

OLD LADY PORN

The Man Cave

He did *not* look good in the crotchless, black lace teddy. Especially bent over in the horse stall with a long vibrator in hand.

No, it wasn't a good look at all. His horrified wife backed away and ran across the corral to the house before slamming the door behind her and hyperventilating.

In the years since she'd first discovered her husband's perversion, there had been mercifully few incidents such as this. The kids had still been at home that first time and, after the histrionics had subsided and asinine explanations had been offered up, the couple had come to what was seen as an interim agreement. As soon as the last child left home, they would divorce.

But, over the years, she learned to avoid 'his' territory in the old horse barn, and he respected 'her' territory of the house. They enjoyed a satisfying life of friends, music and hobby cars. When the logical time came to divorce, they had reached an accommodation that allowed them to share what they could and to give each other the space that made such accommodation possible. They felt too old to start over and explanations would be a nightmare.

Why had she now violated their territorial bounds all these years later and charged into the barn? There was smoke coming from it and he wasn't answering his cell phone. Well, the smoke she'd seen from the kitchen window turned out to have been rising *behind* the barn from a neighbor's burn pile half a mile away. And, obviously, he was in no position to dig the phone out of the pocket of pants he wasn't wearing.

For years, she'd been able to put her fingers in her ears and say 'la-la-la' when the fact of her husband's cross-dressing came too close to being voiced. After that first time, they both gave the topic wide berth. She was way too old for this shit.

Again, after an epic verbal battle and a few tense, wordless days, the couple's old patterns began to settle back into place. If you don't have to be confronted by the evidence of it, living with a cross-dresser probably wasn't as bad as what some women she knew put up with. And he felt lucky to have a wife who pretty much looked the other way as long as he put up an Ozzie/Harriet front for family and friends. He wasn't *gay*, he just needed to feel the ruffles.

OLD LADY PORN

It was only a few months later that he punctured his colon with a snazzy new 'rectal stimulator.' The wife was out of town visiting friends for a few days, so he'd grabbed the package off the front step, ripped it open, dressed to the nines and treated himself to staying inside the master bedroom for his frolic. Which is where she found him. By then, he was just barely alive and it was likely that the infection killed him rather than the ghastly wound he'd inflicted on himself.

It had taken a while for his wife to stop flinching when she remembered the abject humiliation of the 911 call and its resulting hullabaloo. Now, a few years later, she's relaxed into a newfound freedom and is a genuine merry widow (and *not* the kind with lace on it).

Leslie Baker

Aunt Bertha
The Can Opener

It was love at first sight. The two strangers stood at the indoor window and watched their respective cars being sloshed and sudsed along the conveyor apparatus of the carwash.

The women appeared to have little in common; one casually dressed and the other a total fashion plate. Tiny and under ninety pounds on a fat day, Athena was, in her late 60's, watching her first-ever (and brand new) car. In *my* sixty years, I'd never been *tiny*, knew a fat day when I saw one and had owned a jillion cars since I was sixteen.

We started talking at the carwash window, moved with the cars to the outdoor finishing area, on to lunch and never stopped talking until Athena died ten years later.

From the carwash forward, a platonic threesome was formed; my husband Chet and Athena were almost as smitten with each other as were she and I. Thanksgiving and Christmas dinners were taken together, birthdays were wildly celebrated, and fun was had.

Oh, and the *learning* that took place! Athena, a recognized Homeopathic practitioner saw the makings of a protege in me while I was happy to share with her my love of gardening and exploring backroads.

Tiny little Athena was one of the ballsiest people I've ever known. She'd been an R.N. who specialized in critical care babies and was lured from her native New England to a San Francisco hospital to help in their department for two years. On her return to Connecticut, she found it felt claustrophobic and opted to move west. She basically threw a dart at a map and hit Vernon, Arizona. This woman was a *total* city person. She had never lived anywhere other than a condo or apartment. Never driven a car and I doubt she'd ever owned *anything* without a designer label, much less a pair of work jeans.

Following the dart throw, she and a friend flew to Phoenix, rented a car which the friend drove the 4 hours to Show Low where they met the real-estate agent Athena had called. The three drove 10 miles out in the sticks to the property which Athena bought that day.

Athena learned to drive, bought her first car, conquered living with a well, solar power and a septic system and

OLD LADY PORN

gloried in her lovely little home and ten untamed acres! She'd lived there about eight years by the time we met at the carwash.

I always drove on our many outings because, as supremely accomplished as she was in other areas, and as bullet-proof as I consider myself, Athena's driving put the fear of God in me. Whooeee. But you couldn't scare that woman. She reveled in the hairiest roads I could find and loved seeing the mountains with someone who had grown up with and loved them as much as she did.

In the years we had together I only remember one disagreement on any topic. Athena didn't believe in vaccinations and I do. Oh! *Two* topics...she made the most exquisitely *beautiful* Borscht you can imagine and just the thought of a beet makes the back of my mouth do the scary thing that sends you running for the john. Other than that, we were in perfect sync on politics, men, coyotes and much else. We'd had such varied life experiences that we were always learning something from each other. Athena was a brilliant intellectual who tolerated my ignorance and forced me to up my game. It was a deep and invigorating friendship.

Athena had never married. She still had a photo of the love of her life who had died before they were to be married many years before. While she had dated sporadically and enjoyed men, she didn't seem to feel the need of a partner.

Chet and I still miss Athena. On some holiday celebrated at our house, Athena had accidentally taken home a container she thought she'd brought. Now, maybe once a year, some little thing (the black handled can-opener or a corkscrew) will go missing around the house and one of us will say 'Athena is at it again'. We both enjoy that short visit as she toys with us.

OLD LADY PORN

The Spat

Every couple has some version of a 'spat' on occasion. For some, it's a dignified, time-out kind of event while others rattle the rafters with their histrionics.

For most of us, the arguments over who put the scratch on the car or forgot to buy coffee can get heated, but they do blow over.

One of the perks of a day or two of slamming doors and bitching at each other is the make-up sex when it's over with.

Is there anything grander? Yowza. The intensity and passion of sex after a dust-up is hard to duplicate. Damned near makes it worth picking a fight.

Enjoy it while you can, youngsters, because it's a fleeting thing. I know how hard it is when you're under fifty to believe that sex will become a distant memory at some stage in the future. Just the thought of it might motivate you, while you're still young enough, to get rich. If you're rich enough, male or female, you'll always be able to buy some version of sexual activity. You can get fat, wrinkled, limp or dry and still find someone willing to jump through your hoops if you have enough money and few enough scruples to throw at them.

There *are* those couples who have been determined and adaptable enough in their sexual relationship to keep a measure of intimacy alive longer than most. For a few years, they feel proud and just a little smug to be the only ones in their circle of friends to still be getting laid on some sort of regular basis. Eventually, though one or both of them gets too sick, too tired or too discouraged to keep it up. (No, that's not a pun.)

If you really are each other's best friend, have a host of topics to discuss and fun things to do together, you can have a happy marriage without sex at any age. But it's more common to have established your relationship with sex as a major component and to discover it gone is to find a cavernous hole to fill. *Also* not funny. It's easy to drift apart as you pursue your own interests. It can feel pretty empty, but there's comfort in familiarity so most couples adapt. Holding hands as you walk across the store's parking lot and sharing popcorn at the movies gives couples a measure of intimacy and reminds them how attached they are.

OLD LADY PORN

Don't ever think, though, as you look around the room at all of the elderly couples at a wedding, funeral or political rally that they don't remember what great sex was like. If you've ever had it, you don't forget it.

Leslie Baker

The Ladies' Writing Group

The women of the writer's group were savaging the work of one of their members when another member broke into sobs.

'Gwen! Honey, what *is* it?!' came the chorus of concerned voices. The four of them began rummaging through their bags looking for fresh tissues to offer their distraught tablemate. Most of the five women didn't even know each other's last names. Their twice a month meetings were focused on editing and critiquing whatever writing they'd brought in that week rather than on socializing.

So they were a little awkward in knowing how to console Gwen, but everyone tsk-ed, went for water, said and did all the right things until the poor woman calmed a bit.

"Gawd, I'm so sorry. That just came from nowhere. Well... I guess Sylvia's story must have done it, but wow," Gwen hiccupped. Gwen was the youngest of the group who were mostly her mother's age, so she often had a different and welcome perspective on the readings than the others. But this was uncharted territory. And got even more so.

Sylvia's story had been a sad and raunchy one about the fallout from a cheating husband's trail of damage. No one had really *enjoyed* it, but a few of the gals could at least *relate* to it as they searched out errant semi-colons and plot holes.

Recovering her power of speech, Gwen went on to turn the two remaining hours into a major therapy session. She claimed to have been in and out of professional counseling for years (but was apparently overdue for an appointment). One of the better storytellers in the group, Gwen was able to keep them all spellbound with her tale.

The narrative began (and ended) with Gwen thanking the women for being the kind of friends who would allow her to actually cry in front of them. "I'm like everyone, I *need* to cry sometimes," she sputtered, breaking into sobs again. "I don't have any friends with any patience *left* for my hysteria. This has been going on for years and the few who have stuck by me are sick to death of it. I don't *blame* them, but what am I supposed to *do*, go down to the city park and cry with the bums?! I need friends who will let me *cry*."

OLD LADY PORN

The other women exchanged looks while wondering what they were involved in. Sure, they chatted while Gwen composed herself again, we all need a shoulder to cry on. Sotto voce: "usually this takes place with your best friend in a private setting, but let's try to be here for Gwen if we can."

Whoa, Nellie, and bar the door! What the women learned (and would play hell *un*learning even if they wanted to) was that Sylvia's story about the faithless man was a pale reversal of Gwen's own tale.

While trying, many years ago, to be something she wasn't, Gwen had gone through an impressive series of failed relationships. Each failure had left her more depressed and floundering as she sank deeper and deeper into self-destructive behavior.

At some point, Gwen had begun cheating on the men before they could do it to her. It started out with manic dancing and drinking binges and devolved into almost compulsive cheating. Of course, this solved exactly nothing, so she drank more, smoked and snorted enough dope to sink a ship and repeated the whole cycle.

It was a difficult story for the four older women to sit through, much less empathize with. Everyone's had issues, but the kind of insanity Gwen was describing was of a variety most of them had never even dreamed of. But they stoically tried to be kind and keep the shock off their faces.

What Gwen had probably thought was going to be the grand finale and blow everyone's socks off was actually kind of a dud.

Gwen was obviously as queer as a three-dollar bill. And just as obviously didn't realize that everyone already knew it and didn't give a damn. In listening to her wrenching narrative, each woman had put two and two together to deduce that Gwen had always been a round hole who was never going to accept a square peg. Because of family or professional pressure or a million other reasons, she had tried to be something she wasn't. Which everyone's done at some point, but this poor woman really took it to its limits.

Maybe having a bunch of unwoke old gals be more interested in her writing than in her gender status will help Gwen relax into being who she is.

The Girl
Such a Bother

It was so exciting! Her first bra! She felt like such a grown-up as she hooked those two little triangles of t-shirt cotton over her non-existent breasts. A few months later, when wearing the damned thing had become de rigueur, it wasn't nearly as much fun.

Who cared if those obnoxious little boobs jiggled around while her horse ran the barrels? The bra was way more trouble because you were always yanking at it even while trying not to. But by now, she was being monitored, so slipping out of the house without it wasn't happening.

Oh, sure it *was* fun to compare bra sizes with her friends who were all vying for the biggest size to brag about while sighing with forbearance at the trials of being a woman. It was kind of a toss-up as to whether it was fun or not when the boys noticed the new apparatus. But it was definitely a pain in the neck when it came to dealing with the stupid thing during a volleyball or softball game.

Nothing was as mortifying as the 'period,' though. Nothing. Oh, the school nurse had been gentle and supportive on the day she called Mom to come pick the girl up from class. But the poor girl was still humiliated as she sidled along the walls of the corridor trying to get to the parking lot without anyone seeing the back of her skirt. She never wanted to be seen in this town again; couldn't they move to Armpit, Iowa? Tonight?

And then! Talk about apparatus. Back then, tampons were in their earliest stages and certainly not anything 'nice' girls were introduced to. No, instead the poor girl was subjected to a 'sanitary belt' with clips front and back holding a huge, gross 'sanitary pad' in place for the fifteen minutes before it was saturated with blood and had to be exchanged for another pad. Yuk. Lucky are the women who came of age after these pads had adhesive that stuck them to your panties. *And* whose moms realized a tampon wasn't going to endanger a girl's priceless cherry.

Moms tried to put a rosy spin on all of this by assuring their little darlings that menstruation was a thrilling rite of passage which conferred womanhood on them for real. Of course, then there was another conversation recapping earlier overviews of where babies come from. Double yuk.

Like some pheromone from hell, all of these changes turned boys into weirdos. Suddenly, the guys she'd competed against in softball, drinking a Coke the fastest without it's coming out their noses, who could spike the ball the hardest, all of that became infused with a whole new vibe.

A few of her girlfriends had completely different reactions to the sexually charged atmosphere than others. Some of them began 'fooling around' in earnest while others still preferred to wrap their legs around a horse. Moms began to discourage friendships with certain girls they'd liked before.

During one emotional spike, the girl screamed to her mom that becoming a woman was way too much of a bother and she wanted to go back to the way things were before.

Years later, as the young woman gently pushed the hair back from her own daughter's tear-soaked face, she remembered her mom's loving words and arms. Many of our transitions in life are made more bearable by realizing how women have been helping girls to *become* women since the beginning of time.

Leslie Baker

Greta in the Spotlight

"*Six weeks?!* Are you *insane*?!"

Obviously, the aging Hollywood star wasn't impressed with the opportunity to be a presenter at an upcoming awards show. She hadn't been the producer's first choice for the gig, but Ms. First Choice had fallen off the wagon during the extensive physical makeover necessary for such an appearance. She wouldn't be released from alcohol rehab in time to finish her physical rehab.

So when Greta's agent took a deep breath and made the proposal to his longtime client, he wasn't surprised by her lack of gratitude. Six weeks isn't nearly enough time for the dieting, lifting, Botox, and crepe-y skin tightening procedures necessary to that three-minute showing on a national stage. Hair, make-up and tooth-whitening are last minute incidentals compared with the full-body restoration that is generally called for.

Leslie Baker

Only so much can be camouflaged by designer dresses, industrial-strength undergarments, and instant tighteners. The rest is work for surgeons. The world's most expensive surgeons. These people earn the big bucks by performing miracles on short notice. Some of the miracles last for an equally short time, but even most of those require at least some recovery period before the recipient can be seen in public.

Six weeks might work for a woman in her fifties who's still working and maintaining on a regular basis. For anyone older, who hasn't been in the klieg lights for a while, it's not doable.

Greta had been a fairly big star in her day. A large percentage of the audience for one of these industry showcases would be orgasmic at the chance to see her again. Even though she hadn't had a starring role in a major film for twenty years.

And those years had taken a toll. High living and low savings had left Greta in the very common predicament of faded movie stars. She was in debt up to her eyeballs, but too obsessed by how things 'look' to lower her standards of living and spending. The idea of an actual payday blotted out the reality that preparing for it was likely to cost more than she would earn in a good year, much less three minutes.

OLD LADY PORN

Like all of these one-time idols do though, she entertained fantasies of a renewal of her career in the aftermath of the award show. She envisioned agents and producers elbowing each other out of the way as they scrambled to her somewhat ratty front door (add 'paint door' to list). She would have lucrative offers to pore through and be back on top in no time!

For one who had cut her teeth on fantastic story ideas that had become blockbuster movies, making the leap from her own fantasies to the possible was cake for Greta. She wouldn't be pissing away good money after bad, but making a shrewd investment in the revitalization of her career. Maybe this would even be her big chance to marry well. This time she'd hold out for money and not be a sucker for looks. Surely there's some rich sixty-year-old who's tired of twenty-something starlets and would be thrilled to escort (and support) a film legend? Stranger things have happened, right?

Yes, this was it, Greta decided after an hour or so of serious reflection. This was her last big chance at the golden ring and she'd be a fool to not grab while the grabbing was good.

Leslie Baker

OLD LADY PORN

<u>Yesterday's Newsh</u>

I'm so excited to have been invited back to the local paper as a columnist! I wish though, that I'd thought to use kneepads rather than wearing holes in my jeans while groveling. Even so, a small price to pay!

Especially when the paper seems to be on such an upswing. The Letters to the Editor section has really picked up in participation recently. I've always thought that it's a great barometer of community interest and maybe involvement, when people actually care enough about what's written in the paper to comment on it. This new vibrancy in the local newspaper makes me wonder if there's a hope that print media might survive, after all.

Speaking of the media, have any of you noticed, in the last couple of years, the growing tendency of speakers on television and radio to pronounce the letter 'S' as 'SH'? thish was bad enough when it began with female anchorsh and commentatorsh, but recently (sometimes pronounced reshently) even shtudly looking men are using it.

Leslie Baker

I'm a news junkie, so those are the programs where I notice this new phenomenon; I don't know if soaps, sitcoms or cooking shows are doing it, too, but I'd be interested to hear.

What would have encouraged journalism schools to add such a stupid affectation to their curriculum? And why is it spreading? What is that course called? Don't any of the agents or mothers of these people mention to them how idiotic it sounds? This posturing is so annoying that, once it catches your attention, it really detracts from the message the speaker is trying to convey. Which is sometimes a blessing.

All in all, journalism is in a pretty sorry state these days. The once hallowed distinctions between news, opinion and entertainment have been blurred to irrelevance. I don't care if opinion and entertainment want to crawl in together but am not one bit happy to see news join in on the ménage a trois. While I'd like to blame social media for this (as well as for the trash truck being late) I don't know if that's true. The amalgamation of what used to be two forms of commentary and one of reportage on the state of things has more of an evolutionary feel to it.

Entertainment and opinion are optional and discretionary; if you don't like that movie or talk show, you can choose a different one. But news should be news.

OLD LADY PORN

You don't have to hear it if it sets your heart aflutter, but it shouldn't change to accommodate its audience. News is one of the few things in life that truly 'is what it is.' To have it shaded and molded to fit what can only be described as a political persuasion is dishonest in the extreme. It's increasingly hard to find unbiased news reporting and that should be a concern to us all.

I wish I could tell you that Yesterday's News was back in a format that Walter Cronkite would recognize, but Walt wouldn't know the news as we see it today. And this column you're reading? It's always a shameless combination of opinion on the news and everything else with no pretensions otherwise. Yell back and enjoy!

Leslie Baker

Duarte

Is Jerrie ever sorry she didn't take him up on the offer? Not as often *now* as she was twenty or twenty-five years ago, but occasionally.

Probably none of us has ever considered an action that would be hugely satisfying but illegal as hell without weighing the possibility of a life spent in prison. Or of *not* getting caught but of having to live with the wholly different person the act would make of us.

If you were to ask anyone who knew either of them back then, you'd be told, without exception, that they'd witnessed a divorce of a caliber usually seen only on the Lifetime channel. It was a doozy and altered the lives of Jerrie, Bill, their daughters and a few friends in ways which still reverberate.

One day, during the brouhaha of the divorce, Jerrie was having her hair cut and in charged her estranged husband. The shop was a very small one where Duarte, the owner, took only one client at a time, and he'd met the soon-to-be-ex a time or two. Imagine his and Jerrie's surprise when the ex landed an obscenely large bouquet of yellow roses in Jerrie's lap, threw himself on his knees and set off on a soliloquy about why they should reconcile. Forget *her* discomfort, can you imagine how the poor hairdresser felt?

As many do in longtime client/hairdresser relationships, Duarte and Jerrie had developed a real friendship and he'd stewed over her well-being. He was a tough guy and had the ex entered in a violent rage, Duarte would no doubt have put a bullet through him. Instead, the nutcase was shooed out as calmly as possible and the haircut was finished.

After the disruption, Duarte asked Jerrie if she was planning on reconciliation. Ah, no. He made clear to her that he recognized this kind of erratic behavior from experiences in his own life and that he was worried for her safety.

Turns out Duarte was tight with the owners of the local refuse firm. This outfit was owned by a family of some local renown. They were generous immigrants who supported charitable causes and liked to have their names out there. They also hired their crews with the proviso that they be violent convicted felons; (at least that's what was surmised after any interaction with them as they emptied the locals' trash barrels.)

On the day being discussed, Duarte discretely offered to arrange for the ex, while out on one of his daily bicycle rides along narrow, hilly, rural roads to have an encounter with one of the behemoth trash trucks.

Boy, *that* would have tied up a lot of loose ends. And if anyone ever *deserved* the thump-thump of a trash truck (with its instant clean-up option), Bill was the guy. Part of Jerrie would love to have had the stones to give the project a thumbs-up but she's free, happy, and glad she didn't make herself a hostage to the past. It's kind of delicious to contemplate, though, isn't it?

Leslie Baker

Aunt Bertha
Infidelity

Infidelity. Yours or his? Or both? Some marriages survive it, but most don't. What's the deciding factor?

Some couples probably decide that the children are at such a vulnerable stage of development that they'll be civil and tough it out until the kids are established in their own lives before pulling the plug. By then, there may be grandchildren in the picture and the couple have reconciled to a degree that allows them to live (fairly) happily ever after.

What sort of accommodation has been arrived at in the meantime? 'Just don't let my friends hear about it and see whatever little whores you need to;' or 'If I ever even *suspect* that you're spreading your legs for some scum, the kids will hear every detail.' How about a civilized: 'We'll smile and be nice to each other until senility sets in and we forget all about it'?

'For better or for worse' may have been coined for situations like these, but the preacher didn't mention that 'til death do us part' doesn't mean that you can shoot the cheating sonofabitch.

Why do some people cheat and others don't? Is it a sense of entitlement by the same people who don't follow any of the other rules, either? We've all known of someone who wouldn't cheat on his taxes yet doesn't mind a fling here and there. Or someone who's as regular a churchgoer as they are a serial philanderer. If your spouse cheats and you know about it, does it give you carte-blanche to do so too?

If you've been caught in a weak, vulnerable moment and indulged in a brief affair, how does it impact the rest of your life? If you don't get caught, decide to put it behind you as a severe error in judgement and try to keep your marriage together, can you? The shame that you can't share with even your closest friend can probably make fundamental changes in who you are. If this change results in a feeling of gratitude that you were spared disaster and a promise to yourself to never again go so far astray, that sounds healthy. But there are so many other ways it can alter a person. Forgiving yourself as you'd forgive anyone but your spouse is probably as realistic as it gets. Spousal forgiveness is so intricate a maneuver it's hard to envision the gyrations involved.

OLD LADY PORN

What about those people whose spouse sleeps with the sister/brother-in-law? (And it's surprising how often this happens.) Boy, talk about being betrayed on *many* different levels! Sure, you can divorce the cheater you married but you're pretty much stuck with the one you were raised beside.

I knew a woman struggling to get out of a terrible marriage when a wonderful guy crossed her path. The timing was bad, but she'd been so demoralized by the situation at home that the interest from someone who was actually nice to her was hard to resist. So, there she was, literally between the sheets with Mr. Nice Guy, when she suddenly couldn't do it. She couldn't consummate the deal; cheating just wasn't who she was. It would have been a perplexed fly on *that* wall when she bolted! This gal did get out of the bad marriage, never saw Mr. Nice Guy again but *did* find another good fellow. I've always liked that story because it shows that you can rise above your situation and stay true to your values if the phase of the moon is *juuust* right.

Of course, the moon isn't always just right, and people make some awful decisions from which it *is* possible to recover. Or not.

Leslie Baker

A Tidbit

She rushed to the arrival gate to meet the lover she hadn't seen in three months. It was a spring evening and she'd driven his ancient pick-up to the airport; it was packed with all they would need for an early season camping trip to one of their favorite spots.

He was mildly surprised to glimpse her over the crowded arrival area. Why was she wearing a black trench coat and high dress boots to leave for camping? Who cared? He was way beyond caring about her clothes except for getting them off of her in the shortest time possible.

As they met and fell into a passionate embrace, she whispered to him that she had nothing on under that coat. *"Nothing?!"* he blurted. "Not a stitch" she flirted audaciously with him. It was quite a sight watching him make his way to the baggage carousel while trying to conceal the front of his pants with a laptop.

The short trip to the parking lot and piling into the truck was filled with hilarity and joy. Getting away from the airport and out of the city to the first dark road they could find was a challenge of trying to keep at least one hand on the wheel. The road they chose *was* dark, but having the door open to facilitate the gyrations involved meant that the old truck's dome light shone brightly. He jimmied his leather wallet into place to block most of the offending light.

This was a quick and dirty affair conducted by two people who had been desperately pining for each other. As they finally collapsed into a messy, sweaty heap and tried to catch their breath, they became increasingly aware of the smell of something burning. That had been some seriously hot sex, but *smoke?* Really?

The dome light had burned a substantial hole into the wallet before he was able to extricate it. He kept that wallet for several years as a fun reminder that always brought a smile to his face.

Aunt Bertha
Baby Mania

The woman hollered 'whoa,' let the reins drop and squatted in the furrow to give birth. After packing herself with the cotton cloth she'd brought along that morning, she wrapped the baby in her shawl, tied it on her chest and slapped the mule's back with the reins. The plow, the mule, the baby and the woman moved on with their day.

While that may be an apocryphal version of the story, it's probably closer to what that farm woman would recognize as a look at childbearing than the one she'd see today. Forget the midwife, this gal certainly got through the process without a doula, lactation doula, postpartum doula, labor coach or any of the other aides and assistants crowding into today's Labor, Delivery, Recovery, and Postpartum rooms. Even a woman who gave birth in the 1970's or 80's can feel like she's entered a time-warp when looking at the rituals entailed in the process as it plays out now.

Leslie Baker

From the day the impending birth is announced on social media to, apparently, the day that baby signs up for Medicare, every moment of its life is shared in excruciating detail and glowing photos on multiple media platforms.

Many of the accouterments that pour in as gifts for the newborn are totally unrecognizable to those whose children were born in much simpler times. The planning of the young parents' lives around the baby from the point of realization forward is a concept foreign to those who, no matter how thrilled they were to welcome a child into the world, kind of just went on with their lives. People expected the children to adapt to the schedule of *their* lives rather than turning the scheduling over to the tiny dictator.

The years before a child starts school are the freest ones that parents will have until that kid heads for college and to cede them is to give up five years you'll never get back. To feel that you can't leave your baby with a sitter for a few hours here and there or with willing grandparents for a couple's vacation might not be doing your marriage or your child any favors. It's never too early to teach a baby that the world does not revolve around them. Sure, love them to pieces and share their lives with joy, but don't give up the other aspects of your life that make it *your* life.

OLD LADY PORN

Doing things as a family and knowing that there's always a parent available to them is important in raising a confident, secure child. But just because you can't wait to post a picture of your child with Mickey Mouse or have him experience the zoo, don't expect him to *remember* any of it if you do it too soon. While it's probably an exaggeration, I've often said that you might just as well lock the kid in a closet until he's seven or eight if your goal is to have him to remember all of those fun experiences. Maybe looking at photos years later will convince him that he really *did* meet Goofy, but he's not going to remember very many of the early events that were so much fun for you to choreograph. If *you* want to go, by all means make it a family trip, just don't hold out a lot of hope that it will make the highlight reel in his young brain.

My niece was taken on a long trip to the San Diego Zoo as a toddler and the only thing she showed much interest in were the chickens wandering around. They were familiar from the family farm, I guess, but the girl has no recall of the expedition.

Spending obscene amounts of money on baby equipment and clothes might make parents and their friends feel that they're doing right by their child, but I suspect that I'm not the only Auntie who looks askance at the whole spectacle. I wish my Mom was still alive so I could ask her if she felt this puzzlement as *her* kids began to reproduce. Did she and Daddy look at how my sisters and I were raising our babies and think the world had gone to hell in a handbasket? If so, they were as circumspect in their mutterings as I'm *trying* to be.

Online Dating

Lola's problem was that she was so damned photogenic. In her late 70's now and recently widowed, she was getting ready to jump into the pool (or swamp) of online dating and had to have a profile photo. The one taken at her granddaughter's recent college graduation party is a great picture of her, but she could never live up to it in real life. So, what do you do? Put one out there with all of your chins and age spots on display?

Almost as problematic is the profile itself. At this age, a person has a lot to choose from. Do you want to emphasize the Lola who attends meetings three days a week with groups committed to doing good works? Fosters homeless dogs for the pet shelter? Volunteers at the library? None of those descriptions tell how often it's sheer grit that gets her there because she's in one sort of pain or another. Or has a hangover. Or is out of incontinent undergarments and can't risk wetting her pants in public.

Then there's the Lola who loves working and entertaining in her garden. But do you want to tell potential beaus that you can't haul a bag of manure over your shoulder anymore and are considering moving to a facility where everything's maintained for you? Which of these Lolas is the real one?

When considering these and other either/or choices for describing herself to online possibilities, Lola has to bear in mind that all of *them* are going through exactly the same weeding-out process in forming their *own* narrative. We're all so many people by this age. And most of us are a different person at 9am on a good day than we are eight hours later the same day. On a bad day at the end of a week encompassing several trips to different doctors for varying ailments, a dating profile would not be a pretty picture.

Many of us don't want to be alone after the first year of widowhood or of having been abandoned for someone thirty years younger. But bringing a real, live person into our lives with their own seventy plus years of issues is daunting, too. Sure, you can be giddy with the feeling of a new romance after all these years, but when looked at with a cold eye, it's pretty damned scary.

But still, we consider signing up for an online dating site. If you want to find a partner to share your vintage

OLD LADY PORN

Porsche and trips to all of the club's activities, there's a site for that. Or for old real estate junkies. Readers and writers, cat or dog lovers, hikers and bikers, drinkers and thinkers. Name almost any niche you can think of and you can find someone who shares your passion. Unless your passion is sexual. If you're old enough to be reading *this* book, you're old enough to know that sex is a one-woman activity no matter what those wanna-be Lotharios online are promising. Oh, sure, there might be some initial bone-jumping, but don't count on it's being a steady feature in any relationship between old folks.

There are several ways to approach online romance. You can leap right into enthusiastic chat on any number of topics while being as scintillating as you dare and doing so in your bathrobe. If you have no intention of ever getting together with any of the guys you 'meet' online, go ahead and use your very best photo and be the Lola you've always wanted to be. Just remember that most of the fellows you're chatting with are doing exactly the same thing. This can be fun for a while and get you back into thinking like a sexy, single person, but most women burn out on it quickly.

If you're actually looking for a real person to share the Porsche passion with you, you have to be a lot more careful. The fellow who says he only lives 40 miles away and sounds really great may always have some excuse for not meeting at the bookstore for a cup of coffee. He probably weighs 300 pounds, has a wife and lives in Timbuktu or a correctional facility. Meet a person immediately in a safe, public place if you think you want to follow up for real. Don't ever lend him a dollar and don't let him know your address. This venture can be as intimidating as it is exciting.

Lola specifically stated in her profile she didn't want to meet any Republicans. And don't you know that the most persistent fellow she met *was* one? They had a fun fling and he nipped at her now and then until she pulled the plug, but what gives with *that*? Forbidden fruit? One contact, after she revealed her true identity (on the third dating site she tried) turned out to be an old friend from grade school. They lived hundreds of miles apart and he was in poor health, but they enjoyed trading stories about their hometown and the people they knew in common. Another fellow was a retired farmer from a nearby area and when Lola met him for lunch, she found a lovely old guy who was sad, lonely and way too much of a project for her at this stage. Just what she needed: to let herself feel like a fink for not volunteering to look after him!

Lola finally decided on the nicest old folks' home she could afford, met guys in the public rooms there with whom she could flirt and visit, each retire to their own apartments, meet over breakfast the next morning and do it all over again. And if some guy really pisses her off, she can always go back to her computer!

Leslie Baker

The Newcomer

He carried a thick sheaf of papers as he lumbered toward us. The huge polo shirt flopped around him concealing the pistol tucked in the back of his jeans.

None of us remembered having seen him before, although he said he recognized a couple of the writing group and that he'd attended a year or so earlier. As we'd already gotten started on our presentations, the group leader skipped any but the most perfunctory welcome, got the fellow, who introduced himself as 'J.D.' seated and asked the current reader to continue.

As is our custom, after each member's reading, the rest of us offered thoughts on revisions or asked questions to help the writer to clarify a point. The big fellow immediately took part with loud and boisterous enthusiasm. In most of his offerings, he also made a bold assertion that *his* turn was going to be the biggest treat of the day.

Leslie Baker

As the clockwise rotation continued at the round table, I think that we all tried to give J.D. the benefit of the doubt, allowing that he was probably nervous at being the newcomer and having arrived late, besides.

When his turn to read rolled around, J.D. boldly announced that we were in for a real thrill and to buckle up, although he was unsure how much of his (massive) manuscript he would get through. Our group leader stepped in and gently pointed out that we had a plus or minus 1,400-word cap on our readings and explained about how many pages that might encompass.

This direction was not accepted with good humor. As the newcomer fumbled around trying to choose an excerpt, he told us that when we heard what he had at hand, we were going to beg for more. That may have been the first time that any of us shot a quick glance at one another.

The guy was a hell of a performer, I'll give him that. As he launched into his psychedelic story of a drugged-out thirteen-year-old boy growing up in the 1960's, you kinda felt like you'd just dropped a tab and weren't sure where the exit was. And you were *looking* for it. J.D. fancied himself as being along the lines of Hunter S. Thompson would be my guess. *He* was having such a helluva good time himself that there was no *way* you weren't going to sign up for the ride.

OLD LADY PORN

But it wasn't fun. It wasn't entertaining. It was old and sad. It was disjointed, offensive and pointless. And, worst sin of all in a writer's group, it was boring. When our dear leader was finally able to rein the guy in, I think that we were all shell-shocked; not by the story certainly, but by the bombastic delivery and his certainty that we were going to hail him the next Jack Kerouac. There were a few tentative questions and gentle suggestions, but they were met with unveiled condescension and broad hints that we were a bunch of old fuddy-duddies who wouldn't know a good time if it bit us on the ass.

There was one more reader after J.D. but I couldn't tell you a thing that he said. I was unsettled and uncomfortable. Was it just me or did the others feel the dread in the room?

By the time the screaming police and ambulance vehicles skidded into the parking lot of our meetinghouse, we had huddled in a stunned silence in the lobby. As much as we all wanted to bolt and run, we'd been instructed by the 911 operator to stay on site.

The two who had been splattered with blood and dripping brain matter stood there shaking and weeping while being consoled, if not hugged too tightly, by the rest of us. Sobs and murmurs were the only sounds. The shock of what we'd just witnessed was stupefying.

Before being released by the police to try to reassemble our lives, we agreed that whoever *could* make it to the regularly scheduled meeting next month would be there. I at least, was envisioning something of a support-group type of gathering.

It's tragic that a troubled man committed suicide. That he coldly trapped a bunch of unsuspecting folks into being a part of it was without conscience. We'll all carry the hideous experience for the rest of our lives. But we'll never lack for writing material.

The Girl
A Farm Town

Grandad hadn't been dead for very long when a longtime neighbor of his had helped the family to find a suitable first horse for their girl. Curt was a genuine cowboy who always had a horse or two that he was training for others as well as his own working horse, a handsome sorrel quarter-horse named Dutch.

The family had known Curt and his wife Odean for as long as they'd all lived in the small farm town. They didn't have a lot in common or socialize much, but they were friendly neighbors who enjoyed an occasional beer together at the Elks Lodge.

A few years later the chubby, horse-crazy girl had become a skilled rider and Curt began offering her the chance to work on some of his clients' training projects. What a win-win proposition! The girl and the horses learned a lot and Curt scored some cheap labor. Everyone was happy, including the girl's family who were relieved of the constant need to ferry the fourteen-year-old back and forth to the farm to ride her own horse. Curt was happy to swing by and take her the short distance out to his pens.

The day that Curt copped a feel as he helped the girl to mount a new and skittish horse was the day that everything changed.

The girl knew she should tell her folks, but she also knew that it would mean the end to her great horse adventure. She was just getting past the age when a kids' world is so insular that they assume the blame for everything (divorce, death of a dog, family fight) because, after all, they *are* the center of the universe and nothing happens that doesn't revolve around *them*. So, while she put the blame squarely on Curt for being a dirty old man, she also felt that she was tough enough to not allow it to happen again.

When it did, she had to admit to herself that she couldn't take the risk anymore. She told Curt that she wouldn't be riding for him anymore without referencing the reason and was flummoxed when he had the gall to ask why. "You were Grandad's *friend*," she began as her voice failed her, and sobs took over. "I've always thought that he's been so glad to look down and see us with the horses because he knew he could *trust* you to take care of me!"

OLD LADY PORN

As she wiped her nose on her sleeve and tried to choke back her crying, she turned to get in the truck for what was going to be a quiet, tense ride home.

Curt died a short time later and the handling of it was very subdued. If the adults knew any details, they never shared them with the girl. Odean soon left the state to live with a daughter that no one had known they had. All those years of being in that town and not a *soul* had heard of a daughter!

The era was a suicide-prone one. First, this older fellow had killed himself, maybe in shame for having molested more than one young girl and possibly his own daughter. Then another guy with teenagers did the same.

Peggy and her family were in the happy process of packing their 20-foot travel trailer for a family camping trip. While Mom was at work and Peggy at school, Dad and the son were finishing up when the boy, in the kitchen, heard a shotgun blast. The poor kid, just out of high school, ran out and found his father splattered all over the inside of that trailer.

Within a year or two and less than a mile away, a beautiful young woman took all the pills she could lay her hands on. Delightful children and plenty of money hadn't been enough to soften the heartbreak and shame of a cheating husband.

Tree-lined streets in small farm towns aren't the image that comes to mind when you think of violent death.

The girl never told anyone of the line that Curt had crossed with her, but she was pretty sure that he wasn't in Heaven with Grandad looking down. The other families' lives were altered beyond measure and their blips in the girl's consciousness helped form her views on life.

OLD LADY PORN

Yesterday's News
The New Yorker

Late last year, we got an offer to subscribe to 'The New Yorker' magazine for a year for about $12 (and get a dandy tote bag, too!) Sure, why not?

Well... I hadn't remembered that the New Yorker comes out weekly rather than monthly. Sheesh, we're going to have to add another Tuff Shed to the place to keep up with the deluge. This is a periodical for serious readers with endless reading time available to them. While we qualify on both counts, we like books, papers, lots of other magazines, sudoku and other puzzles, too.

Maybe if you feel that all of your news and entertainment needs are met by this one publication (and I suspect that there's a breed of uber-urban coastal dweller who fits that description perfectly) you could digest it all before the next issue showed up. But we've bitten off more than we can chew.

Leslie Baker

At the end of most years when the subscription renewals begin to flow in, we pare down by a couple and it's always a wrenching process. There are a few that are non-negotiable (Smithsonian, National Review, True West, Preservation, Southwest Art) and some that we've dropped and gone back to over the years (Garden & Gun, Sunset, Arizona Highways, National Geographic, Sports Illustrated). There have been some serious errors in judgement, too. Last year I had the foolish thought that, if I had Martha Stewart's glossy coming in on a regular basis, it might inspire me to start cooking and/or entertaining again. Pffft... *ain't* gonna happen! Those days are history.

I can overlook the decidedly left-wing political slant of TNY; I didn't expect anything else and at least it doesn't claim neutrality. This magazine is wholly unaware of (not dismissive of, but oblivious to) those of us out here in flyover country and proudly unapologetic, even smug, about it, so it's not reading material for anyone who can't work around that attitude.

The first 15-20 pages of a New Yorker issue, I can skim through; we're not going to be attending any Broadway productions or dining in the latest trendy spots in NYC or environs. I do enjoy the book reviews and Letters to the Editor (some of which make good points while others are just laughably pompous, an entertainment win either way).

But then. Then you get to the red meat. There is so much seriously good writing in the interviews, articles and fiction! It's easy to skip something written on a subject which, even if penned by Salinger, would bore me, but it still leaves a lot to read. I'm schooling myself to quickly opt-out of writers whose florid style suggests a person more in love with the sound of his own voice than in effectively relaying a story. That *still* leaves a lot of reading.

Certainly, there are worse dilemmas to have and we'll work through this, but pass the smelling salts, I'm feeling vaguely like an overstimulated Victorian lady.

Leslie Baker

OLD LADY PORN

Aunt Bertha
Turning Seventy

The old lady said: "Uh-huh; tell you what, darlin,' you just keep my number and give me a call when you're seventy-two or -five. Let's see how you feel about it then."

I laughed when I heard that old gal counseling the young chick at the gym. Apparently, the younger woman, who appeared to be in her mid-fifties, was a physical therapist helping her older client through some rehab after hip surgery. Fifty is still such a piece of cake! And of course, the PT was fit as a fiddle and couldn't envision herself any other way.

There's a reason that it makes the news when a guy is still doing triathlons at 95 or some woman is rappelling at 100: it's damned near unheard of, is why. The folks who make the papers with their geriatric feats are the exceptions rather than the rule. Sure, they may serve as inspirations to younger people, but to those of us over seventy, they're pretty much an annoyance. They remind us of some of the poor choices (smoking, drinking, late nights) we've made which have us wheezing, wrinkled and out of shape. Or of some of the bad luck we've suffered. But *we're* not in the headlines unless it's on the obituary page.

Seventy years old. It's a fuckin' wall. Healthy or not, fat or thin, straight or gay, fit or flabby; seventy years of age is a wall that will get your attention.

It's astounding to realize that you've vaporized right through that wall like a cartoon character. You glance over your shoulder and see nothing but brick; there's no turning back. It's so unexpected! When you've been strong all your life, you just expect it to last until you wake up dead some morning down the road.

What is it that makes 70 such a roadblock? There are several unpronounceable medical explanations for our physical deterioration, but they boil down to plain old aging the same way your beloved old dog does. One of the more recognizable causes is 'stress.' Well, hell's bells, <u>*stress?!*</u>

If stress is one of the culprits in aging, I don't know how *anyone* lives past 71. We oldsters can't do half the tasks of everyday life without encountering the damned technology which is supposed to improve or simplify things but doesn't. Our well-raised kids and their children are living in such a totally different world than we can relate to that our most important relationships are fraught with stress. Our friends and family are being diagnosed with hideous diseases on a regular basis. And then they die. We're spending money like drunken sailors, but instead of buying a good time, we're buying hearing-aids, new teeth, another pair of glasses, mountains of diapers, prescriptions out the wazoo, or a shiny new wheelchair. Nothing as fun as a sailor's bender. Yeah, there's some stress in being seventy.

If you talk with a dozen octo/nonagenarians who still have enough of their marbles to remember their earliest 70's, eight or ten of them will tell you that things were going along pretty well until they hit seventy, at which point they began hoarding the good days like gold.

So, paste on a smile, grab your walker and get to your physical therapy session while you still can; ninety is just around the corner!

Leslie Baker

Two Notes

If you're reading one of these two identical notes, you're hurt, angry and looking for someone to blame. Whichever one of us was behind the wheel, even if she was soused, is *not* to blame.

All of you probably think you know everything there is to know about the two of us high school buddies who have been each other's most inseparable and precious friends well into our seventies. While we've both made other dear friends over the years, we two share a bond that is, apparently, unbreakable.

And we've put considerable stress on that bond a few times in ways that, if you don't already know about them, sure don't bear repeating here. But our default state of being is as each other's staunchest friend and ally through thick and thin. Through boyfriends, husbands, kids and kin, the two of us are a constant.

You, as our children and siblings, know that anytime one of us is in the hospital, has suffered the death of a loved one or any of life's crises, you call the other of us at the same time you alert the rest of the family members. That's kind of what we're doing with these notes, trying to keep the lines of communication open.

At this stage of our lives, we've both buried more loved ones than we'd like to count. We've watched many of those people try for years to defeat a disease that really had the upper hand from the get-go. Through our varied experiences with others' suffering and death we (as usual) arrived at the same conclusion. Our visions of how we like to think we'd handle the end stages of our own lives are the same. As is our realization that the person ailing and/or dying is often not the one calling the shots. We know that all of you love us and would make decisions on our end game out of love and compassion for us, but, having been in your shoes more often than you have been at this stage of your lives, we also know that disagreements and emotions run rampant at times of turmoil.

Many years ago, (probably in our mid-40's) we began (while only half joking) tossing around the idea of making our future end-of-life exit together. On our terms. Several years at a time would go by when the topic never came up, but then one of us would be facing a possible or real crossroads and would give dispensation to the other along the lines of: 'If I have to bail over this, I don't want you to feel like we have a spit-shake or a blood-promise that obligates you to go, too. You're young and healthy; gobble up your life and remember me with love.' Obviously, whether through laughter, tears or both, we survived all of those test-runs.

We've both had lives that are ever so much better than they might have been. One of our most important bonds over these sixty-plus years of friendship has been our innate understanding of where each other came from. Not only did we know and interact with each other's families, we knew firsthand which of those family members put our friend in danger and which were her saviors. We've always spoken a language that even our siblings didn't have every syllable to; our external reactions to people and circumstances may have differed, but our gut-level knowledge of them was the same. We both feel blessed in the extreme to have landed on our feet and had lives that could have gone so badly south of here.

But now we find ourselves deep into the south end of life. Both of us probably have more physically wrong with us than we're even aware of because we share the same disdain for doctors and their medications. What we *know* about is plenty, though. Neither of us has any interest in existing on tubes and sick from drug interactions. We both have some issues that show little sign of letting up and we're too damned tired to find workarounds. Probably 'tired' is the operative word in all of this. Young people have no idea how draining it is to just get through life at this stage. Things that might have unhorsed you for a week or two twenty years ago feel insurmountable these days. So, you get tireder.

Spiritually, the two of us have been through myriad changes over the years but have (again) ended up in a pretty simpatico place. We're both excited about meeting God and our families on the other side and *really* hope that Satan isn't going to be our greeter instead. Only one way to find out.

A few months ago, when we were on the phone trying to put lipstick on the respective pigs that our lives were feeling like, one of us suggested that she was considering checking out. The other tried to jolly her out of it by saying: "Hey, you can't do that on your own! What about our Thelma and Louise pact?" A discussion ensued about where we really were in our lives and whether it was time for the two of us to take our last drive.

Maybe one reason that movie resonated with both of us so strongly was the driving aspect of it. Both of us are very competent drivers and have little patience with hesitant, lousy drivers. We're about the only people with whom the other can be a totally content passenger for hours on end.

OLD LADY PORN

But we've both seen the Grand Canyon way too many times, so we began to discuss other venues for the big dive. In ending our conversation that day, we promised that we'd each do some research toward identifying a spot without so many safety barriers that we couldn't blast over the edge at 90 miles an hour and bring an end to this great adventure called Life.

Here, we come back to the concept of blame. Neither of us cajoled or nagged the other into something she wasn't ready for. Just the opposite. As time went on, we both got a little giddy at what we were planning, but we never stopped giving each other off-ramps. And that will no doubt be true right up until the accelerator is floored for the last time. So, no blame. We want all of you to continue to love each other and mourn our loss together. We went on our best guess at the right time, we did it in joy for the lives we've lived and relief for the pain we'll avoid. Please hold joint celebrations of our lives and know that all of you were the whole reason that we had such full, joyous lives.

Leslie Baker

I sent this to one of the best writers I know to see if it made sense. Her reply is great:

> *My first thought is that all of your real children and siblings are going to put you both under protective order. And since your friend is unnamed, they all, every one of them, will collectively refuse to ever get into a car with you again. Each one will be wondering if, in a drunken haze, they had agreed to this final act.*
>
> *Hilarity ensues when you finally coax someone, ("Oh, come on, hop in, it's just a story!") into your car, then gun it down a long curvy hill that runs along an unobstructed cliff, hunched over the steering wheel like Golem, mumbling over and over, "...a deal's a deal." And when you're safely at the bottom, you slow down and continue on wordlessly. Now that's good comedy! You will be the talk of the next baby/bridal shower/birthday cocktail/reveal event.*

OLD LADY PORN

But seriously, this was an interesting read. I found myself wondering if this is more common than is known. What IS the upside to eking out the last few despondent and painful years? How many people die in "accidents" of their own design?

You continue to try to call down through the murky tunnel of years to explain to young people what it's really like. As with some other things I've read of yours, I felt like your audience is our children.

How is your second book coming? Can't wait to walk into a bookstore for the reading! ("The author, oh yes, I know her. We have a death pact.")

Now, *there's* a fabulous writer!

Leslie Baker

OLD LADY PORN

The Reason

But why? Asked some of her not-so-close-friends. Why on earth would you end a 20-year marriage to a guy who obviously treasures you? Who surprises you with a Maybach and extravagant trips? Who buys you the occasional piece of jewelry and *not* from Sears? Who provides million-dollar houses? Why indeed?

The friends who interacted with the couple on a more intimate and regular basis didn't ask the same question. Their questions were more along the lines of: What took you so long? How have you put up with him all these years? Did you finally get tired of being the only grown-up in the family?

The wife never knew if the husband had cheated on her; she'd always just assumed not, but you know the old saying about assuming. Even years after the divorce, none of her friends had ever spilled any beans along those lines; who knew if it was just a matter of not rubbing in salt or of there not being any beans to spill? No, fidelity had never been the issue.

Parenting had been the issue. She had gone into the relationship knowing the man had been born into a highly dysfunctional family, but she was head over heels and felt his seemingly sincere vow to never turn into his father could be kept. Besides, they weren't planning on having children, so spreading of familial tendencies shouldn't be an issue.

After a few years of marriage, things were going pretty well and the husband began to push for a child. She loved the guy and they were successful enough in their business that there seemed to be no reason not to, so she stopped the pill and got pregnant.

For a few years, they presented a picture-perfect family: plenty of money, time and friends to enjoy it with and the perfect child.

Oh, there were a few glitches. Like when he became insistent on a second child and totally dismissed their agreement that one was the limit. She'd been over 30 when their child was born, and she'd kept *her* part of the deal. On the day he brought her home about 4pm from having her tubes tied, she found he'd arranged to have friends in for dinner at six. That sort of glitch.

For the most part, though, theirs was a full life of travel, entertaining and feverish work; they both thrived on it.

OLD LADY PORN

She adored her child, embraced the Soccer Mom thing, volunteered to drive on field trips and loved watching her child interact with his friends. Her husband showed up at school and sports events at least as often as other dads did, so it all looked great on the surface.

The major kicker had been his inconsistency with the child and his inability to grasp how damaging it was. He'd punish the kid for doing something one day and then encourage it the next day. Expect independence today and smack the child for it tomorrow. Untold hours of couples counseling never flipped a switch.

He'd gotten to be the same way with her. 'Isn't she beautiful/smart/talented?' to friends at dinner and 'Look how fat/stupid/ clumsy she is' over drinks. Occasional diamonds were supposed to smooth over any hurt feelings.

One morning as the child was eating breakfast and Mom was getting the house ready for the morning rush to school and work, Dad came barreling through and berated her up one side and down the other. She locked eyes with her son and his plainly said: 'Are you going to *take* that?!' 'Ignore it, Baby, he's just being him' was her reply. But it was the end.

She realized that morning that she was going to turn out another generation of rotten men if she and the child didn't get out right then, and they did. The husband's example of how a man could treat a woman was learned behavior and the child had to see that a woman didn't have to live with it.

That's why.

The Botanist and the Writer

"I *did* enjoy the article; thanks for sharing. Not sure why it made you think of me, though."

This was the email response Betts received from her friend Fran after sending the link to a recent magazine article on the life of a 19th century female botanist. Betts' first busy impulse was to be glad that the story had been well-received and let it go. Days later, it occurred to her why it was important that Fran see the connection as Betts had seen it.

The woman from that long-ago era had been both of and ahead of her time. She was intelligent and had married a man who became influential and wealthy at a young age. She did all of the expected things for a socialite of the age: had the correct number of children at the right intervals, ignored spousal dalliances, entertained others of comparable social strata and employed (through her husband's guidance, of course) the requisite number of household help.

But there were a lot of things this Victorian lady did exclusive of her husband's wise counsel. Most notably, she kept her *own* counsel on a great many things. She wrote scholarly books while keeping up with wifely duties. She made time for what was important to her aside from her marital obligations. She was her own person in a time which didn't encourage autonomy in women.

These were the same unheralded traits that Betts saw in her friend. Fran had always marched to her own drummer but was so unobtrusive about it that she tended to be underrated. Her 2.1 children, immaculate home and effortless entertaining would have made the Victorian botanist proud. With her (also underrated) career behind her, Fran was finally trying something that had always niggled around the edges of her life. And it was the first time that Betts had been aware of any hesitation on the part of her intrepid friend.

Fran now had the time and money available to pursue writing a novel rather than the grant applications that she had handled for the local college. Because she knew that Betts wouldn't pull any punches, Fran had allowed her to read a few pages of the budding novel. Betts had been blown away by the quality of her friend's writing! She'd never considered the creative skills that had been honed during those years of groveling for money. Fran was a terrific writer.

OLD LADY PORN

But *she* didn't believe it. Fran kept her aspirations so close to the vest that it was almost impossible to encourage her without feeling that you were intruding. So, Betts took the time to craft a light, gentle email response to her friend: "This is *you*, dummy! *You* are the Wonder Woman of the 21st century! Grab that bull by the horns and show the world your stuff!"

As Fran's novel goes to press, the two women are still friends.

Leslie Baker

Change of Seasons

Only the third week of August and the breeze already sounds like fall. How can a ruffle of breeze *sound* different than it did two weeks ago? As she worked from her garden shed, she wondered if the sounds of fall were metaphorically speaking to her own stage of life as well as to the coming change of seasons.

Last week she and her husband had heard from some friends that they were selling their beautiful acreage and home to move into a senior living facility. The place has become too much upkeep for them as their health deteriorates and they're going to take the plunge. Now that the contracts are signed, reality has set in. They sounded completely terrified at the thought of getting rid of 95% of their possessions, all of their land and damned near 100% of their square footage.

The couples' three children want virtually none of the treasured collections of a lifetime, so the only thing to do is to call in a professional to conduct an 'estate sale' even though they're still alive and kicking. The real-estate guy suggested that, even if they have to arrange a loan, the best way to manage the transition is to get themselves and their few remaining possessions settled into the facility, have him hold the estate sale and find someone to ready and stage the vacant property for listing. In that order. They are devastated and exhausted just thinking about it.

She feels their friends' pain acutely because she and her husband are about a year away from having to face the same dilemma. Every time one of them edges around the conversation, the fear and loathing is palpable. Couldn't they just be that pair of fossilized skeletons that someone finds stretched out in their recliners? Then the whole process would be somebody else's problem.

But winter is coming and decisions must be made.

<u>Aunt Bertha</u>
<u>Does it Have Beds?</u>

After driving all day on that leg of our trip to Yellowstone, our goal was to find a hotel with a bar in which to watch that night's championship boxing match between Evander Holyfield and Lennox Lewis. As we headed north on Wyoming 789, the map indicated that Creston Junction, Wy. was right *at* Interstate 80 and showed a big, cloverleaf interchange connecting the two highways, so we figured it would at the very least have trucker motels; and who likes a good fight more than truckers?

As we arrived at the junction, there it was, the bed we'd been anticipating. Sadly, it was just a rusted old tangle of bedsprings tossed on the shoulder of the 789. And it was the <u>*only*</u> thing except dirt and asphalt for miles in any direction.

So, we wheeled onto the 80 West and sped 82 miles before sliding into a motel in Rock Springs. We bellied up to the bar just in time to hear that the fight had been cancelled because one of the fighters had the flu.

Over the years, Chet and I have travelled many thousands of miles by the seats of our pants and that was one of only three times when we were ever very sorry to have not planned ahead. We almost always plan a route that parallels an interstate by 50 or a hundred miles, preferring to explore small towns, forts or ruins rather than making speed on freeways. While we've had some less than stellar nights along the way, we like the flexibility that comes with making no reservations. We do like to have a *town* there, though.

Another spot that occasionally enters our preplanning conversations is Rolf's. I'm not even sure what state we were in, but northbound along the Pacific Coast Highway or the 101 in extreme northern California or southern Oregon, we began to feel the need of rest. We hadn't even seen any *cars*, forget towns or people for a long time and it was beginning to have a bit of a Deliverance vibe when Rolf's appeared on the left. This winding stretch of road probably saw an hour or two of sunshine in a year; it was dark, drippy forest and Rolf's wasn't exactly a welcoming beacon but it was there.

A one-story string of 5 or 6 rooms was anchored by a small office/restaurant tended by a gal who took us to our room noting that the window didn't close all the way and the door didn't *latch*, but it was a good room and the restaurant would close at 6. Hmmm. She *didn't* mention that the heater didn't work and that we'd freeze our asses off that night.

Eager to get some food while it was still an option, we hurried back to the cafe. The menu had a European slant to it which was puzzling, since you'd have thought that Pork 'n Beans would be about their speed. But it was *fabulous* food! Nicely served and with a good wine, to boot. That and a hearty breakfast the next morning almost made up for the laughably bad room. Leaving escalating banjos in our wake, we blasted north.

We often spend more time planning and anticipating our trips than we actually stay on the road. You'd be hard-pressed to find two people more enthralled with old-fashioned, paper maps than Chet and I are. A few of the magazines that we take offer glimpses of places that become the impetus for a road trip. Out come the maps and yellow legal pad and the fun begins! We find our target attraction and begin checking out everything worth seeing between here and there. Because we avoid cities like the plague, try to always make circle routes and end up in some pretty God-forsaken spots, one of the questions we ask ourselves when we consider a place as a possible stopover is 'Does it have beds?' Creston Junction taught us that a spaghetti bowl intersection on a map doesn't guarantee anything.

A bed in and of itself doesn't guarantee much, either. We're disinclined to pay much attention to the calendar except as it pertains to whether our dear friend is available to pet/house-sit, but the third of our major travel boondoggles taught us to be a little more calendar aware.

We were on our way home from a trip to southeastern Arizona and decided to spend the night in Oracle; back then, a lovely little town and not just a suburb of Tucson, so we were happy that our day's driving would end there. Until we discovered that it was the Fourth of July and there were almost no beds unless we wanted to go back to Tucson with still no guarantee of a room. Instead, we took the last room at The Chalet. It was a dog pit of a place, so we put the key in a pocket, didn't unpack the car and drove all over that hill trying to find another room. If we'd found anything else, we'd have just eaten the cost of The Chalet's room. After finding ourselves winding through a dark neighborhood in San Manuel where obvious gang members made it clear we were in the wrong place and stopping at a Circle K for a snack and being damned near mugged, we slunk back to the pride of Oracle.

OLD LADY PORN

The scorpions didn't even wait for us to turn off the 40-watt light bulb. They (and who knows what else) were all over the puke colored carpet, in the sheets and swarming the shower. We grabbed the few things we'd brought in with us, shook them well, ran to and slept in the car. It was a memorable night.

Like all married couples, we've had our ups and downs through the years, but one of the things that's kept us happily together is that we like to travel in *exactly* the same way. We enjoy the same towns, attractions and scenery. We like about the same number of hours on the road in a day and the same sort of food and accommodations at the end of that day. We both get antsy after six or eight days out and are ready to head for the barn. After a few months, though, the maps and the yellow pad come back out and another adventure begins!

Leslie Baker

OLD LADY PORN

A Tidbit

It had been a grueling day for both of them when she dropped her car off at the repair shop, he picked her up in their little 'fun' car and they headed for home.

Why are you driving Bitsey? she asked. Oh, she needed a wash and I thought we could both stand to unwind a little, he replied. They both just leaned back and enjoyed the music and the top-down ride until she yelped that he'd passed their turn.

Well, we're not going home for a couple of days, he smiled over at her with his Ray-Bans reflecting in the sun. Thinking he was pulling her leg, she just pressed him about where they were *really* headed. Finally, he spilled that they were going up the coast to Mirbeau for a couple of nights.

But what about Arnie? She felt confused about their child's whereabouts. He assured her that their longtime, trusted sitter was child, house and pet sitting for the weekend and that all would be well.

What am I going to *wear?!* What about my toothbrush? My make-up?! I have to go home and pack a bag! He calmly told her that it was all in the trunk, that he'd handled it all. And believe it or not, he had. He had not overlooked one single item that she needed to spend an indulgent, sexy and pampered couple of nights with her husband.

The Longest Affair

"Bullshit. Of course they slept together!" The foursome at the bridge table had been debating this point for most of the afternoon. Now, over cocktails, the salient points were being rehashed.

Last week, the four women had attended the funeral of a mutual friend their age who had lost a mercifully short bout with cancer. Only one of them had ever before met the dapper fellow from out of town who came to pay his respects to Alma.

Susan and Alma, the gal who died, had been lifelong best friends and Susan was the only one in this group who felt sure that her friend had never been intimate with Dapper Dan. The other gals had heard stray references to Dan over the years and had obviously formed their own opinions on the subject.

Dan and Alma had met in their late twenties or early thirties and Alma had died at seventy-six, so theirs had been a long friendship. Longer than any of Almas marriages or Dan's dalliances. Oh, it's probably not fair to call them that; from what Alma had said over the years, Dan was a serial monogamist. And a couple of his relationships had lasted in the five to eight-year range even though he'd never been to the altar. The only woman constant in his life had been Alma.

Like many single men, Dan had maintained numerous long-term friendships with couples he'd met over the years and he and the current paramour were always welcome guests at parties and get-togethers. He and his sweethearts played golf, traveled and lived an upscale life both before and after retirement. They always maintained separate residences even if, in the longest termed relationships, her place sat vacant for a time. The best of both worlds for Dan. And he didn't abuse it; he was generous, faithful and considerate of his lady friends.

Alma's life had been much more conventional. She'd been married, divorced and widowed enough times to raise a few eyebrows, but had lived a respectable life of comfort, friends and good times. Through all of the other men, though, there had always been Dan.

What a titillating topic for these four friends to be dissecting. How does a long-distance liaison endure for forty-five or more years, through husbands and girlfriends and across thousands of miles? Oh, they could pick and prod, speculate and surmise, but with Alma gone, they would never know the truth.

It had always been obvious that Alma loved Dan. When she spoke of him, she sort of lit up and, listening to her, you'd think that he was the most handsome, witty, virile, intelligent specimen of manhood to ever exist. She didn't speak of him often but so casually and securely that she might have been discussing whatever man was actually in her life at the time.

And those men were quickly schooled that Dan was off-limits. The bridge ladies had heard from Alma more than once that some beau or another had been dispatched because of his jealousy over her relationship with Dan. Dan was apparently a non-negotiable part of the package. The men didn't ever have to hear stories about or even references to the third wheel in their relationship, but they had to come to terms with the fact that they'd occasionally overhear a snippet of phone conversation or know that a lunch (*for two*) was planned.

Even Alma probably didn't know the fine points of how Dan finessed their friendship with his lady loves. All she knew was that she could have phone, email, text or personal visits with Dan whenever it was convenient for the two of them. She had met some of the women in his life a time or two during their involvement with Dan.

Alma was always just accepted as an old, dear friend and there had never been anything but a good time had by all.

Not every gal (or guy!) is programmed to accept such an arrangement gracefully.

What, exactly, *was* that arrangement? From what Alma's best friend Susan was able to relay to the group, the relationship had been as pure as the driven snow. There had been a few times over the years when one or both of them were between affairs that they had come seriously close to having a sexual relationship. Maybe because of timing or distance, a consummation had never happened. Or maybe both participants so valued the connection as it was that they were unwilling to risk losing it.

Especially after laying eyes on Dan at the funeral, three of Alma's friends were unconvinced of the chastity of the affair. He was an elegant, masculine fellow who seemed to be mourning the loss of the love of his life. That he knew a little something of each of them said a lot about the depth of his connection with Alma. He not only remembered Susan from their one long-ago meeting, but also from the call she had made to him recently.

Alma had declined to have Dan come to visit her at the end although they'd had long phone conversations. And

Dan had wrung from her the promise that she would ask Susan to contact him immediately when it was over.

This seems to have been a fully requited love affair, with or without a physical component to it. That two people were able to maintain a deep, undemanding, fully satisfying bond for so many years is a rare treasure to be held close to one's heart.

Leslie Baker

Aunt Bertha Lookin' Good

Wow! You look great today! What did you *do*? I can't quite put my finger on it, but it's *working* for you!

Don't you just love getting such a comment from a friend? What you probably *don't* love is having to answer:

"Jeez, thank you, but the reason my boobs are back up where they were forty years ago and my waist has shrunk by six inches is that I'm wearing a brutal back brace for the third day in a row."

There may still be old ladies out there who corset-up by choice, but most of us who never sported underwear more demanding than Spanx wouldn't dream of *Spanx,* much less a corset, these days. When I was in my teens, you had to have a girdle to hold up your stockings but by the time the 1970's rolled around those things were on the trash heap along with most bras. Oh, we still wore pantyhose and proper support to the office Monday through Friday, but it was the '70's and wild 'n crazy described the 'real' us!

Now, those of us whose girls made the boy's tongues hang out fifty years ago envy our friends whose endowments were more modest. Having to worry about getting a nipple caught in your elastic waistband is annoying. They don't make over-the-shoulder-boulder-holders of sufficient strength to haul those puppies back up where they belong. These days, there's not much demarcation between boobs and waist, waist and belly, belly and thigh and on down as far as gravity can take you.

So why do we still try to put ourselves in presentable shape before venturing out? It seems just bred into most of us to try to look our best. Whether we're attempting to lure that handsome widower, working to keep our own handsome sweetie from straying or not wanting the ladies at Bridge and Bunco to 'Tsk' over how we've let ourselves go, it's an ongoing maintenance marathon. And for what?

After a certain age, you're never going to get laid again no matter how nicely put together an old lady you are. Those young, swinging dicks will never swing your way again. What a pisser.

OLD LADY PORN

Why not go ahead and get an easy-care man's haircut at the barber (for a fraction of the price of a hairdresser), forget about those extra twenty pounds and quit shaving your legs? You can still be neat, clean and tidy so that the kids and grandkids don't shun you and people in line with you at Walmart don't wrinkle their noses. Giving in to the fact that our femme fatale days are behind us could sure make life simpler. And cheaper!

Gosh, besides saving all that money on our hair, we with smaller bazooms could just wear wife-beater undershirts instead of bras; we could all save a bucket of money by using witch hazel and glycerin for our skincare; our wardrobes could be pared down to things that are actually comfortable; we'd need so much less in our handbags...oh, it's just dizzying to think of the freedoms we'd have!

So, why do so many of us plan to go to the grave with a trendy hairstyle, exfoliated skin, mani-pedied, and wearing the prettiest incontinence underwear available? Why do we keep ourselves enslaved to the strictures imposed on us when we were still in the game (and you *know* the game I mean)? I have no clue.

Maybe it's harder for those of us who loved sex and all of the games surrounding it than for we who just did it because it was expected and don't miss it in the least. If being a sexual player was never really a part of how you defined yourself, maybe it's a lot easier to get that crewcut and clean out your closet. Maybe if you're the gal who still enjoys a vibrator (since that's all you're getting these days) you put on the strut for Buddy? Lots of 'maybe's in there, but I feel pretty confident in saying one of the myriad answers has to be that some of us were sexual creatures and some weren't. And that our responses to being old and on the shelf have more to do with that than with wanting to impress the ladies at the library.

OLD LADY PORN

The Girl
A Hitchhiker

Just as the radio reception was fading out before the long drop down into the canyon would blot it out entirely for an hour, the seventeen-year-old girl saw a hitchhiker.

The Mamas and The Papas blaring, her black German Shepherd in the backseat with tongue and ears flapping out the window, her '62 Corvair humming, the girl was enjoying life when she spotted the stranger with his thumb out. She pulled into one of the last wide spots before the canyon got serious and said 'Sure!' when the clean-cut young man stuck his head in the open window and asked if the dog was friendly.

Of course, Daddy had told her not to pick people up, but *he* did it all the time, so she never really took his warning too seriously.

This girl had learned her confidence behind the wheel by racing friend's cars on impromptu drag strips out past the

Leslie Baker

Gila River and driving Hansen's flatbed hay-hauler between Lakeside and Vernon as soon as her feet would reach the pedals. Cars, dogs and horses she could handle; why should roadside men be any different?

The first few miles were taken up with figuring out where each of them was going; she'd be turning south at Florence Junction and would let him out there so he could catch another ride on into Mesa. Then there were quite a few very quiet, white-knuckle miles while the girl hurtled through the canyon and the stranger prayed, not always in silence, if 'Oh, God!' counts as a prayer.

When the road straightened out around Seneca, the young fellow began to regain his power of speech. After a couple of perfunctory observations about the challenging road and the dog's good sense to lie on the floor, he said he had something to tell the girl.

"You're young and pretty and you should never, ever again pick up a hitchhiker. You don't know a thing about me, and I might be a killer."

He continued; "My uncle was supposed to drive me down to Mesa where I'm meeting a group to leave on my Mission. But Uncle had to take Aunt Katie to the hospital and I had no choice but to thumb it. I couldn't miss the bus. I shouldn't even *be* in this car with you, but

OLD LADY PORN

I know I'm not going to hurt you and I was desperate for the ride. But please promise me that you'll never pick up anyone again."

She made and kept that promise to a total stranger.

Leslie Baker

OLD LADY PORN

Yesterday's News
Of Barriers and Warning Labels

The Phoenix paper recently published a Letter to the Editor from a very concerned fellow. You could just see his furrowed brow and feel his hand-wringing angst regarding the idiots who fall over the edge at the Grand Canyon. The writer felt that the rest of us should pay for barriers that would mar the beauty and grandeur of the place but would keep morons from falling in while they take their selfies.

I'd like to (ever so tenderly) suggest to this gentle soul that this is a perfect example of Charles Darwin's theory of natural selection.

In the last fifty years or so, we've somehow come to believe that we can and should be protected (by the government in most cases) from ourselves. That, maybe if we make enough laws and erect enough barriers, nobody will ever again have to take responsibility for their own poor decisions. Our lives are filled with warning labels, reminder tones, caution lights, alarm bells, and all manner of danger signs, most telling us things that we used to rely on common sense to bring to our attention. Yes indeed, that table saw can and will cut off a hand if you lay it out there, and if you take a power cord into the hot tub to charge your laptop, you'll be the one getting the charge. Do we really require red plastic 4x6 inch labels to point this out?

If we actually do depend on all of that tsking, what does it say about the people we've become? Nothing good, I'd posit.

Whether it's a warning label on a power tool or a barrier at a scenic overlook, it's pathetic that we're such dithering dunces that we can't feel 'safe' and 'protected' without them. In the first place, the people who most require being protected from themselves are the ones least likely to read and heed warnings. Secondly, each of us, through our taxes and elevated prices, pay for every single cautionary or protective device and sticker out there. Third and most important is the basic fact that, by requiring and funding all of those safety measures, we're circumnavigating one of nature's most basic laws.

Survival of the fittest is a maxim that dictates exactly what it says. If you're past the age of having your parents watch over and instruct you and you're so damned dumb that you can't stay away from the edge of the abyss or out of the lion habitat, then I don't think that we need your contributions to the gene pool. From man's beginning, plenty of us have shot from the womb as simpletons and too many of the slow among us have always reproduced, is it really necessary that we promote the multiplication of fools by cosseting them?

Darwin thought that the individuals best adapted to their environments are more likely to survive and reproduce. Well, stupidity isn't among desirable traits for either survival or reproduction. Let's not encourage it.

Leslie Baker

OLD LADY PORN

Poor Little Rich Girl

More than once the young woman had heard on the grapevine about some well-off local guy getting a divorce, set her cap for him and lost out. She tended to be a little obvious.

It was hard to see why she felt the need to put herself in those circumstances. She was attractive, had a decent education and seemed to fit in with the small city's higher social circles. God knows she could hold her liquor; and those rumors that she'd taken on the whole football team in her far away college? No one had any proof of that. Settling into life as a banker and waiting for the right guy to come along of his own volition would have seemed like a good path.

Finally, one of those newly freed, much older mover/shaker types stumbled into the right bar on the wrong night and was caught in her web. It was a short courtship and a huge wedding. An heir was soon on the way just to seal the deal.

Happily ever after? Not exactly. Oh, she was thrilled to abandon her brief career and be able to devote herself to the golf course. Her tan was supplemented by a second home in the Caribbean accessed by hubby's small jet. *He* was invigorated to have her much younger friends around to impress and flirt with. Some of those friends were more discreet than others when the flirting evolved into short, fiery affairs.

Ten days after the seven-year cap on the prenup had been met, the woman drove a hundred miles away to talk with a divorce attorney. She'd never even have been able to pay the lawyers' outrageous fee with her salary at that eight-to-five bankers' desk and now she should be able to walk away with millions.

Except. Except that she had underestimated how wily her older husband really was. Guess he didn't accumulate the big bucks by being dumb as a rock. No, the lawyer informed her, after he and his team combed through the inch-thick sheaf of papers, there was no sunset clause in the prenup. After the seven years that she'd had in her head, a divorce would entitle her to alimony which was only about twice what she'd have been making on her own by now. She could survive, but the lifestyle would be so radically different that she couldn't even wrap her head around it. She'd been envisioning half of everything! The day dragged on with her questions becoming more

OLD LADY PORN

pleading as the news just got worse and worse. She was stuck.

If she chose to become even more of a deranged bitch than she'd already turned into, *he* could leave at will and only be obligated to give her a stipend, but *she* was fuckin' stuck. Really, her only option was to outlive him.

Even though her husband seemed older than God's wet nurse to *her*, he was only in his mid-sixties and could have another thirty years in him. She'd have had to be stupider than she was to not consider ways to off him. But, according to the attorney, there were some gray areas in even that unvoiced option. How his three adult children and she and their daughter would divvy up the spoils in the event of hubby's death would require more study.

She was already concerned about how she was going to explain the hideous charges on her credit card for the lawyer's retainer and fees. Probably not a good idea to add even more to the tab. She'd used the card which rarely got scrutinized because there was nothing on there but clothes and lunches; with luck, his bookkeeper would never notice.

There are all kinds of cages, some are gilded.

Leslie Baker

Kleenex Friends

What a gift it is to have dear friends. What would any of us do without someone to help us carry the burdens at our lowest points and rejoice with us at the heights?

Mel treasured her friend Vera; they shared everything. From bitching about their daughters-in-law, as they couldn't with anyone else, to recipes to questionable jokes, nothing was off limits. Almost from the day they'd met through the book club, the two friends had bonded. An affinity for the same authors and types of books had given the friendship a great start.

The day came when Mel sent an instant message telling Vera all the gory details of the ill-fated cruise she'd just returned from. Some awful plumbing issue made the boat uninhabitable and it had docked to allow everyone to catch a plane home. Not the idyll that she and her husband had been anticipating.

Several days later, while checking Facebook, Mel was surprised to see no new posts from Vera and realized that her last message hadn't been answered, either. Wondering if she'd been ghosted or unfriended, Mel checked the chat section of their book-club website and several other sites she and Vera also frequented. Nothing new there, either. Twitter messages went unanswered

Vera could be dead or incapacitated. What a shame that would be. But that's the way it is with online friendships; there's really no there there, it's just a way to brag and bitch. You can commiserate if you're in the mood and change the subject back to *you* whenever you like. Few of the far-flung participants exchange phone numbers and they certainly don't know of any family members to contact. Most grieving families aren't going to put in the time, effort and passwords required to notify a plethora of total strangers that their online 'best friend' has kicked the bucket.

These friends are as indistinguishable and disposable as tissues.

So, move on to the next best friend; they're less than a dime a dozen in the online world.

OLD LADY PORN

Aunt Bertha
The Golden Anniversary

Fifty years! To say nothing of sixty or seventy years. Holy smoke. To those of us who've reached old age with a trail of dead or discarded spouses behind us, getting an invitation to an anniversary party marking a milestone like that is almost inconceivable.

What a commitment. Only death will part them, just like we all said in our vows the first time. Who knew you were supposed to take it that *literally*?! For subsequent ceremonies, some of us may have prudently left out the part about death being the only thing that would part us. If we've had enough experience with curvy blond sluts, emptied bank accounts or black eyes, making yet another relationship contingent on death for its termination is a non-starter (or *way* too tempting.)

How does it happen that a young woman actually does wait until her wedding night to sleep with the only man that she'll ever sleep with? In seventy years? Or even fifty.

It boggles the mind for many of us. And makes us feel like we've totally failed in the marriage sweepstakes. Maybe *unrepentantly* failed, but still...

What did these women know that the rest of us *didn't* know? Did they just hit the jackpot and pick the perfect guy right out of the chute? Did they make compromises that we would have been unwilling to make? Did they have other options?

It's easy to say that there are always other options, but if someone's hitting the half-century (or longer) mark in a relationship, then they went into it pretty young. If they had lots of children, moved around the country, or *didn't*, had a religious and supportive *or* a religious and censorious family, any number of factors could play into the options available to a young woman.

There are 'golden' couples who seem content and happy to still be together but many of them have some wrenching stories of what they've endured if you look beyond the fifty candles on that cake. Other couples, while having certainly had their ups and downs, never dealt with infidelity, death of a child or any of the other tribulations that can be deal breakers. Or, miraculously, they faced those traumas and dealt with them successfully. And some couples seem to have been locked in a battle of wills right from the beginning and both were

OLD LADY PORN

too damned stubborn to call it quits. But here they all are, along whichever path. Pretty darned impressive, isn't it?

Leslie Baker

Aunt Bertha
A Ship of Fools

This morning, I saw a reference in one of our way-too-many magazines to the '...burgeoning Incel Movement.' Huh? Yet another trend has gotten underway without me? I read all of those periodicals, watch the news and flip through the occasional newspaper trying to stay abreast of the world and it just keeps spinning on without my consent! *Now* what?

As it turns out, I'm an inadvertent member of this heretofore unknown subculture. Lots of you probably are, too. 'Incel' means 'involuntarily celibate.'

While the genesis of the online group was a lonely, straight college girl trying to connect with others in the same boat, the boat has apparently been commandeered by angry men who can't get laid because they're jerks.

You and I know that there's yet another boatload of us queued up to pirate that ship again, don't we? Gray-haired pirates married to men with erectile dysfunction of some variety. Did you know that the first signs of LDS (no, not Mormonism, but Limp Dick Syndrome) usually appear around age 50? So, just about the time that we women are through with childrearing and menopause and ready to storm that gangplank, the guys in our lives are jumping ship. Of course, some of them limp along for another 20 or 25 years, but they're definitely not standing tall by then. That just sucks, doesn't it?

And suck is the operative word in most geriatric sexual relations. All give and no take gets old fast so, usually, a detente is called, and *nobody* gets their timbers shivered. If that doesn't epitomize Incel, I don't know what does.

So, don your eyepatch Matey, hoist your sword and salute your new crew of Incel shipmates! Arrrggghh!

OLD LADY PORN

Mom and Brad

Mom, for the luvvachrist! I can't put my face on this tripe. I'm sorry...that's harsh; it's not bad *writing* but if we're going to write mysteries *together*, they can't be old lady and cat ones. What if I end up on TV promoting them like you used to? The jig will be up.

Bradley, I see your point just like I did the *last* time we had this discussion, but that's all I know *how* to write. You saw what happened when I tried turning the cat into a surly Swede and the old lady into a slovenly, foul-mouthed detective! I can't *do* that kind of chemistry and it really *was* tripe.

Mom, we've *got* to find a way to make this work and make a living. After taking four years off, I've missed my window. The rest of the faggots out there flexing their stuff for the catalogs are younger and fresher; I'll never get back in.

Baby, I'm so sorry that I've ruined your life.

Jeez, Mom, don't go into that Mom the Martyr schtick again. I'm doing what I *want* to do but we just have to find a way to hone the process. I'm dumb as a rock, *you're* the one who can make your brain do something new and different, not me.

Honey, you're not dumb and you know it. You're a great *editor*, you're just not a writer. And my stuff *has* to be edited, we both know that. There's no reason we shouldn't be a great team. I *still* think that the Dolly Dammit's would sell with a handsome gay 'author' promoting them; I'd only have to change her name and just keep writing. Lorna Leaveit? Susie Stoppit?

Seriously? And shall I show up with my hand on my hip and a limp wrist, too? I *do not* intend to become the 'former model' pet fag of the week on the ladies' daytime shows!

Brad, honestly. Look at the dichotomy you could present! Go out there as macho as you can muster and spin a yarn about how your late mother's stories *just come to you unbidden*. You have no *choice* but to set them down as her voice from heaven dictates...yada, yada, yada.

Mom, why won't you just let me *edit* if I'm so good at it? You write it however works for you and let *me* change the cat to a surly Swede?

OLD LADY PORN

Bradley, you don't get that the *atmospherics* are really altered in trying something like that. That's like your always asking me to come back to life as a freak! It just plain doesn't *work*!

Mother, you are not a freak. *Millions* of people get through life every day with a few scars.

A few scars!? Is that what you call this?? Hair on half of my head? A face like hamburger?! A few fucking *scars*?? I was a beautiful woman five years ago and you think I would even *consider* putting myself out there looking like *this?!*

OK, let's try to de-escalate this a little, Mom. It was *your* idea to commit suicide and I will be truly and honestly grateful to you for the rest of my life. Your note did a masterful job of keeping me out of prison for the wreck. But don't you think that if you showed up alive and well, they'd let me off the hook on the main charges and figure that my having been your caregiver all this time would work like 'time served' on the others?

A] That's not a chance I'm willing to take and, B] Unless we can *earn enough* to pay for a ton of plastic surgery, I will never be seen in public again. Why do you keep thinking that I'll change my mind on that? Not gonna happen. I'm as ugly as a monkey's butt. The only thing I can do is write books which appeal to a certain demographic. If you would just work with me on this, I could make us a living even dead.

Give me a minute here, you just gave me an idea!...How about this, Mom?... Lemme think, here...What if I get in touch with whatshisname...your old editor...and float out there that I've stumbled on a bunch of your unedited manuscripts on a hard drive I found somewhere? Could we massage *that* into a plausible cover? It would make perfect sense that those would still be the Dolly Dammit's you wrote and that I would be the one promoting them! Wow! This might be the answer! Paychecks and plastic surgery, here we come!

The Girl
Faith Finds a Way

From a distance, it would have looked like a pagan ritual taking place in the wooded clearing. The young, beautiful woman, arms outstretched, whirling in wild circles, her long red hair trying to keep pace as her naked breasts jostled exuberantly.

While there may have been some negotiation with gods and spirits going on, the whole hive of bees attacking the woman were having none of it. Some of her co-workers were deep into their own wild and stripped-down gyrations while others tried frantically to flap shirts and parachute cloth at the whole spectacle.

For Faith, landing on bee colonies was only one among the many perils of being the lone woman in an elite firefighting squad who jumped from helicopters to man otherwise inaccessible hotspots during forest fire season. The work took a helluva tough person, male or female, and Faith was one of few women who even tried it in those years.

In her first seasons with the forest service, Faith had manned remote watchtowers with few human visitors through whole fire seasons. Highly ethical and disciplined, she was also something of a loner who loved to read and hike, so the work was a good fit for her. She had, but rarely told, wonderful stories of wildlife encounters and other experiences which could leave her less adventuresome friends agog when she wasn't so stingy with them.

One tale she did share with her closest buddies was of the Outward-Bound expedition on which she was a counsellor. The planned weeklong trek with the young teens to the top of one of Colorado's Fourteeners was stopped at 12,000 feet by an un-forecast blizzard that kept them all huddled for warmth in one tent for several days making it impossible to intercept their food supply delivery. It's a harrowing story in many respects.

Both starvation and death from exposure were looming possibilities by the time the storm lifted enough to allow the group's shoebox-sized radio to broadcast their location out to the search parties. Once the famished group was found, food and blankets were air-dropped to tide them over until the teams could reach them.

OLD LADY PORN

In Faith's family, the rules of the dinner table were 'company is served first,' and she was appalled for years to come by her own elbow-stabbing to get to the peanut butter sandwiches as they plopped to the snow-covered ground. She also remained perplexed by which of the other councilors on the team had become dithering, weeping and useless during the crisis and which had bucked-up and done the hard work. She said she would not have called it right at all.

One wondered if this tale escaped the usually reticent Faith because it had been such a profound encounter with her own mortality. For a confident, capable person to have confronted her human frailty would have been a rare experience for her.

Tough as nails as she was, young Faith had a great ability to laugh at herself. One winter she and two close friends were on their way to a rustic, isolated ski lift. As they turned off the icy main road (such as it was) onto the final unplowed leg of the trip, Faith said to the driver "I have lots of backroad driving experience," offering to drive from there on up if Gail was uncomfortable with the conditions. Gail was happy to hop out in the middle of the un-trafficked road and let Faith take the wheel. They all roared when the car ended up in the ditch 200 feet later, but luckily, at the time they were a great looking trio of young gals who had no trouble flagging down the next truckload of strapping young men to yank them from the gully. All three women have been delighted to laugh together over the incident for the last 50 years.

In her seventies now, Faith and her husband of almost 50 years hike with their rescue dog daily and have a full social calendar. Theirs is a life of spirituality, good wine, books, friends and great memories.

Dream or Intuition?

Sherry lurched awake and out of bed in one motion. As she stood there in the dark, trying to get her bearings, her hand was pressed dramatically against her chest as she steadied herself.

A dream. It was only a frightening dream but one that eventually presented a peek into the spiritual.

This dream began with an accidental butt-dial to Sherry's dear friend Abby's phone. Ab is always a bit on the spacey side, so at first her disjointed, erratic conversation didn't sound any alarms. But as she continued wandering around her house and commenting on off-the-wall topics, Sherry tried asking some questions which Ab didn't seem to process. At one point, Abby handed the phone to her husband, Will. Willy is always an excellent conversationalist and rational as they come.

But Will was dazed and irrational, too. Suddenly, it clicked for Sherry and she told him forcefully to get outside; to gather Abby and their dog and get the hell out of the house and across the street. Sherry found her husband and told him to keep them on her phone and talking so she could use his to dial 911. Emphasized that they _not_ go to the car!

Sherry figured that there had to be some sort of gas leak in the house for them to be acting this way. As she was speaking with the 911 operator, a terrible thought crept up. What if this had been intentional? What if years of deteriorating health had finally caught up with Abby and Will and they'd entered some pact to end it all? What if, in a stupor, Abby had just answered the phone out of habit? Christ. And here I am, making things worse for them, Sherry thought.

Later, when she was fully awake and caffeinated, Sherry called Abby to relate the stupid dream. There was a moment of silence before Ab answered in a hushed voice. Abby told Sherry that she and Will have been a little concerned recently about whether or not the gas log-lighter in their fireplace was working correctly.

Yesterday's News
Tractors and Pigs

On Tuesday, as we stood with our coffee looking out the kitchen window at the perfect, clear morning, Phillip commented that it looked like a scene conjured by Disney. Artist that he is, my husband can be a little theatrical in his observations, but this one was spot-on.

Our colorful birdbath was surrounded by two does, a young buck, some bunnies and a plethora of vibrant birds. Chipmunks scampered at the base of an oak tree closer to the house. It was magical.

This morning was just as beautiful but a little less magical. Two wild pigs/Javelina were near the birdbath. Everyone we know has seen the damned things around here, but in the ten years we've been in this house, this was our first time. Not that we've never dealt with them before. In 2003, as we left California to return to my home state, we hadn't even hit the freeway forty miles from the house in Three Rivers when the realtor called to say that the pigs had dug up the two acres of 'lawn' there. Life in the country, as they say.

I never want to live in a place where I don't run the risk of occasionally dealing with pigs or getting stuck behind a farm tractor for a few miles of highway.

Being brought down to 15 MPH while on your way to something 'important' is a great way to force yourself to take a deep breath and spend those few extra minutes thinking about what's REALLY important. And one of my most important quality-of-life gauges is that it be a rural life.

We were visiting recently with some friends from Taylor who, like us, are always thinking that they're going to pick up and move to that place with the greener grass. The older we all get, though, the harder this place is to beat was the general consensus. That may have been an easier sell sitting outside at 80 degrees, sipping cocktails in the shade, surrounded by summer's colorful bounty than had it been 10 degrees and time to shovel snow.

But I've never minded even our harshest winters. We have such polite snow! It doesn't hang around for months on end becoming a gloppy, disgusting mess the way it does in wetter climates. You get the childlike joy of

OLD LADY PORN

'Snow! Yay!' and the next day is bright and sunny with the snow mostly gone.

I once lived and worked where you had to keep the block heater on your car plugged in 24/7 during several months of the year. If you didn't have that option, you had to go out every little while to start and let it run for a bit. To go grocery shopping, you had to have an extra set of keys so you could leave the car running and still lock it; all of those running cars caused dense ice fog to form over the town.

No, this IS the place with the greener grass, pigs and all!

Leslie Baker

Aunt Bertha
The Holes in the Story

My generation is among the oldest to be living with gay marriage. By 2015, when the U.S. Supreme Court legalized it, most of our parents were gone and we had kids and grandkids of our own. Our parents had heard some of the saber rattling, but never thought it would amount to anything. For my Mom's generation and much of mine, the subject was so unwieldy that it was easier to just ignore the whole thing.

What we got by doing so was the loss of the oldest institution in history. By the time the Bible was put together, marriage was a two-thousand-year-old tradition. And we've managed to undo it in fifty years.

To our kids' generation, gay marriage was a foregone and unremarkable conclusion.

Sure, there have been gays as long as there have been people. Today, like other minority groups, they're living in halcyon days of less discrimination than they've ever known which is something that we can all be proud of.

But marriage? People of my generation and earlier who married in their church of choice made vows with the clear belief that God was blessing their union of one man and one woman. Regardless of our political or religious differences, most people believed in some version of 'one man, one woman'. That defined the word marriage for hundreds of years.

To have that belief ripped from one of their most sacred vows by the inclusion of a group of people condemned in most religions as the most abject of sinners is a terrible injustice to the people who were too timid or politically correct to stand and claim marriage as their own.

I'm as much of a sinner as the next person and am certainly not going to appoint myself to judge too many of my fellows. (Although, do note that 'judgmental' is NOT a four-letter word.)

I don't care if you're as queer as a limp pencil. I do care that gays have heartlessly usurped the institution of marriage so treasured by most of their grandparents.

We were all built (by God, nature or your creator of choice) with an assortment of apertures and appendages

OLD LADY PORN

with specific design purposes. Most of them have a basic in-out function. Sound in/sound out; pollen in/pollen out; baby in/baby out; food & water in/food & water out. Now, you can pervert anything; (who doesn't know of some kid who put a bean up his nose or in his ear rather than in his mouth?) Perversions are called that for a reason, though; they go against our design parameters.

Kids make mistakes because they're kids and have to try most things once. Adults who selfishly put their perversions ahead of thousands of years of religious or societal custom are contributing to the downfall of that society.

Leslie Baker

OLD LADY PORN

Well, You Asked

Following a long, comfy silence as they drove home from a shopping trip, Connie asked her sister (out of the clear blue sky!) "If he dropped the new wife and asked you to go back to him, would you?" It took Cleo only a second to adapt to the non-sequitur; balls from left field weren't rare with this sister of hers.

"*Hell*, no. Hey, do you remember that bumper sticker I had right after the divorce? 'I still miss my ex, but my aim is getting better'? Like that." Forget that the one-time couple had been divorced for almost 30 years and both had been married to others for almost that long. Where does this stuff come from? It had been a vicious divorce with no real hope for reconciliation even then.

"But, for years you said he was the love of your life, don't you feel *anything* for him now?" Connie asked. Cleo reflected that this may be more of a peek at one of Connie's own lost loves but didn't pour any salt. "Y'know," Cleo replied, "I go for weeks or months at a time without thinking of him at all until I hear of some rotten thing he's done to somebody I care about and then I *detest* him with some of the old passion. Does that count as feeling something? Oh! And did you ever see the one that said 'I got a dog for my husband. It was a fair trade'...I loved that one!"

The Love of My Life. What a loaded phrase. By the time we're old, most of us have one who pops to mind at its mention. He may have been totally inappropriate, too nice, too rotten, too something, but he was That One. If off-the-charts lust was one of the hallmarks of the relationship, would you have missed *that*? *Hell* no. A few of us are still or finally married to him, but it's kind of rare.

Having the love of your life behind you doesn't mean that you'll never find true love again or that you wish you had *him* back in your life. If you're smart, you realize that having him back would also mean having back the same old problems that broke you up in the first place. With every passing year, he's angrier, more bitter and hardened and certainly not the feisty young stud he once was. No, the gals who fall for his still abundant charm are much more likely to be spending time on their knees than on their backs. Right after the break-up you may have wished that he'd died so that you didn't have to know he was still drifting around the edges, alive and kicking. Now, you can feel smug that you got while the gettin' was good and that he's someone else's problem. There's a lot to be said for being happy and free; no amount of money or social standing is worth having to tolerate a jerk on a 24/7 basis.

Having *The One* buried in your history also doesn't negate other, much more suitable and enduring loves, in the least. You can treasure your new husband and the life you've built together and never look right or left at other possibilities. You love him dearly with no 'buts' attached. Men are kind of like shoes; at this stage in your life, you're happy to have a comfortable pair that never gives you any pain. You adored those stiletto, candy-apple-red, needle-toed Louboutins and feel lucky to have had a time in your life when they fit right in. Yeah, it was a wrench when they had to go to the consignment shop, but you were on to another phase of your life. Like that party animal who was hung like a horse, who cheated, lied or gambled, the shoes had to go.

In Cleo's case, the only fantasizing happened when she saw her rich, obese ex-husband waddling out of a restaurant as drunk as the slut in tow and beat to hell by poor life choices. "Yeah, Baby? You want me back?" she purrs in the dream, "Start crawling and don't let these tall red shoes catch you in the chin while you're groveling." What fun!

Leslie Baker

Starting Over

Those last few weeks had been brutal. She'd thought that the last few *years* had been as bad as it was possible for life to be, but the end had been worse.

She was abashed when she remembered almost hoping to find him peacefully dead in their former guest room which had become his room. The Alzheimer's had gone on for so long that there was nothing else in their lives; neither of them were the people they'd been or would ever be again.

Theirs had been a wonderful second marriage with children on both sides grown and raising successful families of their own. They'd had time to fulfill a lot of bucket list items and enjoyed their retirement years doing great things together.

One was more intellectual and the other had abundant artistic sensibility. They shared traits of capability and kindness. Their strengths had nicely balanced the weaknesses of the other. Thank goodness that she was an organizer with a head for numbers; full-time caregiving needed that.

After his diagnosis and descent into the hell of dementia, they'd gone through all of the incremental adjustments that everyone in such a situation experiences. She became accustomed to not knowing who he'd be from one hour to the next and to whether she was going to be the beloved caregiver or the money-grubbing bitch who was plotting to kill him. Even after Hospice came into the picture to take off some of the strain, it was never-ending.

A young person expects to parent their children and to help their own parents to navigate old age; youth gives them the happy strength and resiliency to fill those rolls. An elderly person with issues of their own is ill-equipped for a seemingly endless position as nurse, chauffeur, nanny, gardener, housemaid, handyman, warden, laundress and cook to the person who used to be their partner in life but is now an exhausting responsibility.

She'd still loved the 'him' he had been and who could be seen momentarily now and then, but much of her time had been spent in twenty-four hour a day care for a complete stranger.

When the end came, the initial shock was more that it was over with than that he was gone. For the first few weeks, she was more stunned than grief-stricken. The grief would come later. She would be surprised that the silence of her home had a lonely, hollow sound to it.

It was time to start over, but hard to know where to begin.

Leslie Baker

OLD LADY PORN

Aunt Bertha
Peeing

What? You can't have a Greyhound? They've always been your favorite drink! And no diet grapefruit soda, beer or a hundred other things that make you wet your pants?

By the time we're in our sixties and beyond, a lot of women have (if they're lucky) been told by their doctors that, if they don't want to be wearing any of the discreetly named 'incontinent undergarments,' they're going to have to stop ingesting *anything* with citric acid in it.

Wow, we drop those things like a hot potato, don't we? There is nothing more mortifying than to have urine running down your leg (unless it's number two) before you even realized you needed to go. At that stage, we'll all give up anything it takes to never have it happen again.

It's damned near impossible to avoid citric acid, though. It's in everything but mud and milk. And you never have any idea how much is in a particular product until it's too late. It's in many beers, most soda-pops, lots of sauces, juice drinks and other places you'd never before have thought to look for the cursed stuff.

While we're all different, I'll tell you how I keep drinking my favorite summertime libation. I dissolve 1/4 tsp. baking soda in a 2oz bottle of water with a dropper and put in about a dropper-full per one can of soda. Keeping this little bottle in the liquor cabinet allows me to have grapefruit soda with vodka AND dry pants. Though it's certainly possible to get too much baking soda in your system, even *I* don't drink *that* much! Google says, "The recommended dose of baking soda considered safe for an adult is 1/2 teaspoon dissolved in 4–8 ounces of water every two hours" and we're talking a fraction of that even if you drink all afternoon.

This little nugget came from a webpage which also addresses treatments for cystitis. Sigh. Did any of you ever end up in the ER with a punishing bout of cystitis brought on by a long weekend of screwing your brains out? Once is all it takes to learn that indulging in that sort of rowdy behavior *must* be accompanied by cranberry juice. Boy, those were the days, weren't they?

Back to peeing, which, sadly, is more relevant to our lives these days than screwing. Here's an idea to share with your 50-year-old daughter because, if we'd all started doing it *then*, we'd be in better control *now*. While you're on the john, practice starting and stopping the stream. If you're already having control issues, you may have to get mostly finished before you can do this, but if you remember this exercise most times you sit there, you'll be surprised at how much stronger your muscle control gets and it can help to keep your pants dry.

Y'know the little wrist-twist gesture that indicates the twisting of a knife in an old wound? I experienced one of those recently when I'd just barely made it to the bathroom because I was too damned stubborn to interrupt my crossword.

Before I was even seated, I felt my mom giving me a loving little wrist-twist from Heaven. (Yeah, I know none of us like to think that our dead loved ones 'watching over us from above' means they're peeking at us _all_ the time. Most of us have been creeped out by that visual at one point or another.) But this was personal between my mom and me.

One of the first times my mom had a wet-your-pants event in my presence, I wasn't as compassionate as I should have been because I was totally flummoxed, and she noticed. I'd give anything to have that stupefied moment back. But it does make me smile when I can feel her giving me a little elbow nudge as I race for the john.

The Girl
High Morals and Low

Things hadn't gone as planned for the girl who had been raised in a large, religious family and was of the highest moral standards.

The first problem was that the guy she married at eighteen was a dead-end street not endorsed by her parents. Oh, he was cute and Mr. Personality, but with his high-school jock days behind him, he'd pretty much peaked. She was not the type to put up with a weekend drunk who was never going to amount to a hill of beans, so after two years, she divorced him and set off on an adventure in Tahiti.

Tahiti turned out to be more precarious than planned and she returned home in a leg cast. After bunking with her best friend for a week, the ex came calling and, in spite of those high morals, the curtain fell, time passed, and a baby was on the way. So, the one-time couple moved back in together, the baby was born, the ex reverted to his old ways and she dumped him for the last time.

Soon, a great job offer comes through a friend who lives 2,500 miles away and the girl gives adventure another shot. She and the baby set off in her 1967 Mercury Cougar on cross-country jaunt which results in wonderful experiences and a new love. By the time she realizes that the new beau isn't looking for real commitment, she's saved enough to finance her return trip across the country in the Cougar that's got some hard miles on it by now. Sad as she is to leave Mr. Wonderful, she's excited about getting back home and sharing her toddler with grandparents who haven't seen him since he was an infant. She scoots through the Midwest right ahead of the oncoming winter.

Her luck runs out though, in southern Utah. As the weather becomes a full-on winter storm, she decides to power on through hoping to get far enough south to be out of the snow that her car wouldn't be able to handle for much longer. Highway 89 isn't anybody's idea of good winter driving even now and in the 1970's it was worse and even more sparsely populated than today.

When the Cougar breathed it's last, the girl waited for as long as she could, running the heater until the gas ran out, for someone to drive past. Finally, she felt she had no

OLD LADY PORN

choice but to swaddle her child and carry him through the blizzard to an intersection she remembered from a couple of miles back. They would die for sure if they just sat here in the now frigid car.

Miraculously, she hadn't gone more than a few hundred yards when she saw headlights. The old pick-up slowly approached, and the driver yelled that he couldn't stop or he'd never get his traction back, but if she could dive in, they'd give her a ride. She maneuvered herself from the center line onto the passenger side while carefully jogging to keep up with the slowly moving truck. Righting herself and the baby after a headlong and graceless launch into the cab, the girl looked over in appreciation to thank the obviously drunken louts. They weren't interested in thanks. They leeringly made it clear what her fate would be as soon as they got down their own road a little way ahead. The two of them had been on a beer and booze run for their buddies waiting at the house and arriving home with these playthings would be a bonus.

With nothing but the baby left to lose, the girl clutched the child tightly, wrenched the door open and tumbled out of the slowly moving truck. The deepening snow cushioned their fall and neither the girl nor the baby were more than shaken up. But now what?

Leslie Baker

Before she had time to pull herself together, another set of blurry headlights appeared from the direction in which the drunken would-be rapists had disappeared. Oh, God, were they coming back for her?

Crouching behind a scroungy, snow covered shrub, she tried to see if it was the same truck approaching. Finally... no, this one appeared to be newer and less beat-up, so she girded herself for the possibility of yet another nightmare encounter and staggered out onto the road. She was so exhausted and terrified that only the hope of saving her child kept her from giving herself up to a snowy but undefiled death on the roadside.

After initially passing her by, the driver braked as slowly and carefully as possible, the truck began to back up and she braced herself for the unknown.

Two men. But her baby was still breathing little puffs of icy air, so her only choice was to press on. "I turned the heater to high as soon as I saw you," said the passenger as he scrunched himself to the center of the seat. She crumpled over the baby, sobbing in gratitude and relief.

The two fellows explained that they couldn't get her to town in this weather. Their house was just up the road and their mom would be glad to put the baby and her up for the night. Which is what happened.

OLD LADY PORN

The Cougar really had died that night, but the living, breathing girl and her baby were soon reunited with Mr. Wonderful who had realized that he wanted his little family back on a permanent basis.

The girl married him and he adopted her baby. Forty-five years, another baby and five grandchildren later, the girl and her family all thrive in the desert southwest with scant interest in snow.

Leslie Baker

A Tidbit

The fellow was doing the couple a favor by agreeing to meet them at the rental return yard at 10PM so they could drop off the enclosed trailer that had moved the last of their possessions from one side of town to the other. They had a little over an hour to kill before ten and were starving, so pulled into a nearby Mexican restaurant.

Chips, salsa and a couple of beers later, they were relaxed enough to begin planning where things were going to go in the new house. They told the waiter to bring two more beers and they'd stop back by for real food after the trailer was delivered.

As they headed back to the truck and trailer, they began to fool around and decided to make one last inspection of the fully empty trailer. Not the most romantic place they'd ever rendezvoused, but it had seemed private enough until they exited to an appreciative crowd cheering in the parking lot.

Leslie Baker

Yesterday's News
The End of the New Yorker

So. Did you read, last year, my saga of trying to find time to read The New Yorker magazine? The end of our $12, introductory, one-year subscription is finally at hand.

I end the year feeling like I've been dragged through a keyhole. The constant, hamster-in-a-wheel feeling of "OMG, I have to finish this issue because the next one will be here any minute!" has become an annoyance. TNY's proud and unceasing hatred of our President (and our country?) has grown tired and repetitive. The tendency of some of their fiction to morph into porn has begun to feel sly and tacky. More and more of the famous cartoons have become smugly indecipherable rather than tart and funny.

I overestimated my willingness to disregard the political dogma of TNY. I have Liberal friends and we usually find topics on which we can agree and converse. I'm not out to convert anyone and don't expect my opinion to always prevail. I do like to be thrown the occasional bone, though. And that's a concession that is *not* going to come from the folks at Conde Nast. I (very!) reluctantly dropped my long-standing subscription to their Vanity Fair magazine twenty or more years ago when they could no longer discuss a shade of lipstick or a romantic comedy without turning it into a political screed. It's certainly their prerogative to play to a particular audience, but I'm not in it.

There were a few things over the course of the year's TNY subscription that I shared with others, but not enough of them to justify the time expenditure and ongoing political pimping involved in perusing it.

When I first received the proudly logo-ed canvas tote bag that was part of the enticement to subscribe, I had the thought that I might use it and be perceived as cosmopolitan and wide-ranging in my political views. As I'm neither, it never felt appropriate to indulge in false advertising, so I'm hoping that someone who picks it up in St. Vincent de Paul's thrift shop will find a use for it.

OLD LADY PORN

The Christening

The christening water had barely dried on the baby's head when his grandmother excused herself from the sumptuous surroundings.

When Grandmother Frankie returned from her car a few minutes later, the opulent gala was in full swing with Mimosas flowing, happy music playing and giddy people beginning to queue up to the lavish catered buffet. The young couple always treated their friends and family royally and were thrilled to welcome their long-awaited son to life's party.

Frankie worked casually through the room stopping every few steps to hug and accept congratulations from old, dear friends. When the nanny bustled past with her wailing grandson, Frankie couldn't resist a moment of snoodling him before he was whisked away. What a delightful chaos!

A hush began to follow Frankie as the revelers slowly realized where she was headed. One of the beautifully appointed tables already held a few people with their buffet bounty and of course, John was always the first one to the food, so there he sat, holding court. By his side, to Frankie's immense satisfaction, sat his trophy wife. Never a beauty, Nelly had been statuesque twenty years ago but now that she'd gotten as wide as she was tall, all the jewelry in town couldn't camouflage thighs and hips that spread over two banquet chairs.

John's once considerable influence had begun to wane as he neared retirement and, since power had been his primary attraction, the number of sycophants surrounding him had also begun to ebb. Which made it easy for Frankie to approach him.

The two of them hadn't exchanged ten words in these twenty years following the ugliest, most vicious divorce any of the people in this room had ever seen. The spectators held their breath.

The beads from her small, elegant cloth bag flew everywhere as Frankie put a bullet through the place where John's heart should have been. He didn't *have* one, but he was still just as dead.

"Oops!" Said Frankie nonchalantly. "And I *liked* that bag."

OLD LADY PORN

While most of the merrymakers would have been content to throw a tablecloth over John and nudge the party a bit to the left, there's always one poop who has to panic and dial 911.

Payback's a bitch. Frankie hadn't thought of her ex-husband for years except as it concerned their son. On the few occasions that the son or one of Frankie's friends mentioned his father, it always gave a glimpse of a man who felt diminished by his son's accomplishments and a life that didn't rely on the father's largesse.

As hurtful as John's refusal to have an adult relationship with his son was, the young man continued to hope that there would be a light-bulb moment for his father and that they would forge a new bond. Maybe this baby would flip the switch.

But no. When John and Nelly condescendingly accepted the invitation to the christening party, they'd made it clear that it was the social, rather than the familial, aspect that attracted them. They wouldn't even bother to pretend.

Frankie simply refused to let this go on. If she stayed disengaged and let the two men sort it out for themselves, there was the possibility that her son would be the one goaded into killing the son-of-a-bitch at some point. No, it made more sense for her to do it. With a colorful mental-health history behind her, Frankie surmised that, if she couldn't sell an 'accident' she might be able to sell crazy.

The 'accidental discharge' of a gun carried by a woman known to wear her NRA cap to the most inappropriate of functions might have been less acceptable to the local prosecutor's office had the victim been almost anyone else. But when all of the witness' statements and forensics were in, the only charge filed was for misdemeanor accidental discharge followed by a slap on the wrist.

And they all lived happily after.

Thick and Thin

You know that couple who everyone invites to everything? The ones who are so damned nice, fun and genuine that everyone wants to be their best friends?

Donna and Jeff are that couple. It's hard to imagine anyone finding a lousy thing to say about either of them. They've run their local business for years with the utmost integrity; they will jump through hoops to do kind things for their friends and charitable things for their community. They make most of us feel like scuzzbags for not living up to their example.

And *fun?!* Those two define the word. Even in late middle age, they'll try anything once, enjoy a few drinks and yet have never been known to go over the line with any of their antics.

In the last year or two, though, people have begun to notice that Donna and Jeff aren't accepting very many invitations. At first, it just seemed that Jeff wasn't showing up for poker as regularly as usual and Donna didn't do lunch as often. It really got kind of glaring when they didn't hold their annual Fourth of July extravaganza without offering any explanations. Any questions asked of either of the couple were met with cheery brush-offs about how busy they'd been.

Finally, Donna's best friend, Shelly wouldn't take another no for an answer and insisted that Donna come over to her place for lunch and a visit. The afternoon got off to an awkward start; it was obvious that Donna wanted to keep things on a superficial level and equally obvious that Shelly was having none of it.

After one of the pregnant pauses in the conversation, Shelly said, "Jeff has changed, hasn't he?" Donna did all of the evasive what-how-do-you-mean stammering until she wound down enough to nod her head quietly. Shelly put her arms around her friend and cooed while the tears flowed.

Long before the socially active couple had begun to withdraw, Shelly had been attuned to the fact that Jeff had a dark side that was successfully shielded from their more casual friends. But Shelly knew an explosive temper when she glimpsed it and could see that Jeff and Donna had reached an understanding, spoken or not, that this was their little secret.

OLD LADY PORN

It was a delicate threading of the needle that Shelley maneuvered in letting her friend know that *she* knew but no one else in the friends' circle did. She knew how important it was for Donna to show no disloyalty to Jeff. She also knew that heavy burdens unshared are killers.

As old age began creeping up, Jeff's once rare explosions of anger had become more frequent, lengthy and unpredictable. He had always been able to control them to the extent of keeping them out of the public eye. His sunny persona was the only one that anyone but Donna ever saw. But after experiencing brief moments of Jeff's temper in public venues, the couple began to withdraw.

Was Jeff just losing his longtime mastery over his demons as he aged or was it senility gaining jurisdiction over the situation? Appointments, tests and medications loomed in the couple's future. Decisions about how to move forward in the life they'd built would have to be made.

The positive thing to hope for is that medications which might have helped years ago will be found to be effective now and the wonderful couple will be able to resume the life they've loved. If the outcome is less satisfactory than that, though, Donna will have the comfort, support and understanding of a best friend who will be there through thick and thin.

Leslie Baker

OLD LADY PORN

Aunt Bertha
In The Year 2525

I feel like an Indian.

Are any of you old enough to remember the TV commercial featuring an elegant, tearful Native American fellow ruing the desecration of his land by plastic shopping bags or some such scourge?

His ancestors probably felt the same way when rowdy, newly American frontiersmen barreled across the land taking possession and changing its face. Conquest of territories not formerly their own has been man's nature from the beginning and the vanquished have always had the same choice: adapt, die or move on. Not a cozy, politically correct picture, but real life.

Now, it's *my* people who are being vanquished. Humans of all colors and ancestry are being stripped of our territory. Oh, the square acreage isn't changing, but our world sure is. We've now got genders which weren't a twinkle in anyone's eye fifty years ago, 'marriage' has become a term correctly used only by plumbers and *now* we're also being battered by the future.

Much of the entertainment aimed at young people is dystopian in nature and we've begun to see that vision creep into mainstream advertising as well. The same ethos is certainly popular in movies and video games. While some of this content (which kind of eludes us oldsters) is punctuated with catchy music and bright colors, the dark, robotic nature of the genre is prevalent.

You never see, in these augmented reality portrayals of the future, Grandma's old Oriental rug, the armoire handed down for generations or anything that isn't slick and hard. I guess, if the 'people' depicted are the lone survivors of a cataclysmic disaster which wiped out every single thing but them, having mementos of the past is the least important thing on their minds. But, oh my God, is this *entertaining*?

Have we raised our young people to believe they must prepare themselves for a life with no history? To constant upheaval and battles for survival? To no joy?

We already see the pervasive influence of the droid culture in how our homes, cars and communications are run: Siri, Alexa and Ring are monitoring and directing

OLD LADY PORN

large swaths of many lives and their reach grows by the day. Something as simple as a paperback thesaurus or dictionary is already laughably outmoded. Yet, pick one up and thumb through it for two minutes; the mind-expansion you will notice is from letting your mind go outside the bounds imposed when you just ask Siri for a synonym. To envision a world without such marvelous, freeform, learning for the sake of learning experiences is heartbreaking to me.

What are all of those plastic pseudo-people constantly battling for? The chance to curl up by a fireplace with a good book and a nice wine? With Dad's ship-in-a-bottle on the mantel? I suspect not. And yet, in my lifetime, we've come alarmingly close to accepting that hideous vision of the future. I also envision such a future as a world returning to the middle ages when only the wealthy had or could read books.

Or paper maps. As cars become more autonomous, people rely increasingly on whatever mapping system is installed to get them where they're going. Or not; there are some funny and not so funny foul-ups that rural folks see their city friends caught up in when trusting Google to navigate country roads. Paper maps give you a more complete picture of what will actually be entailed in your journey, but they're a thing of the past.

I wonder if it's comforting to young people to know that the Global Seed Vaults in Norway and scattered around the world, are storing viable seed varieties so, once our decimated planet shakes off its nuclear shroud, whoever's left can start farming again? Really? Is that supposed to give us solace when we think of the future our grandchildren are facing? How are preppers holed up in Idaho supposed to even *access* those seeds, much less have the resources available to bring crops to fruition? I'd suggest they make room in those seed vaults for the *books* no one will have time to save as they flee the apocalypse. There won't be any Alexa left to answer their questions on how to farm, so the survivors may have to opt for more low-tech solutions. And city kids whose only interactions with nature come from a visit to the nearby zoo? I'm sorry, folks, but those kids are toast.

People who are thoroughly toasted in the nuclear or other holocaust portrayed in entertainment venues will certainly be the lucky ones. None of us who rely on our talking cars to guide us from point A to point B have any concept of, much less preparedness for, the post-apocalypse.

So, I guess this is where the entertainment value comes in. To see such a future looming challenges young people to fight back, to see a way forward. When you're young, challenges *are* exciting! Whether it's a horse no one else can ride or a mountain that hasn't been climbed, it's invigorating to be The Winner. And maybe there's no other way to look at the future portrayed in movies and VR headset games without becoming complete doomsayers.

I'll take the book, the fireplace and a barrel of wine.

Leslie Baker

A Meaningless Gift

"I need a lovely, totally meaningless gift for someone I don't like," Beth explained to the clerk. The experienced saleswoman nodded sagely and led Beth to the right department.

Leaving the store with a sumptuous, weightless nine-foot long silk scarf for the Canasta group's upcoming gift exchange, Beth considered the recipient and why she grated so.

Maybe it was that Beth felt she saw through Carla's dazzling, ever-present smile to a less glossy 'real' self. Most of the group had been together enough years that they had a pretty accurate insight into each other's good points and bad and liked them anyway. They were a companionable bunch who shared their stories. But the considerably younger Carla *had* no down days, no issues with husband, health or weight; never even broke a fucking fingernail, apparently. Everything was always wide-eyed, gleaming-smile glorious.

Well, you don't have to be the type to spill your guts to be likable, but being a plastic cut-out tended to put some people on their guard. Carla had chosen to follow the 'everything's perfect' playbook rather that the 'let-it-all-hang-out' one. Not a bad strategy, certainly, but more people than Beth were also becoming quietly uneasy with it.

Carla and Beth hadn't hit it off right from the beginning, so last month's conversation with Carla's stepdaughter had only confirmed, not changed, her opinion. Jenny, the stepdaughter, and Beth knew each other through a couple of clubs they belonged to rather than through Carla. Carla's husband (Jenny's father) was significantly older than Carla, meaning that Beth, Carla and Jenny were fairly close in age

On Tuesday, when their accounting work for the Women's League had wrapped up, Beth and Jenny decided to stop in for a drink before heading to their respective homes. After settling in, Jenny asked, point blank, how Beth could *stand* to be around Carla. Trying to walk that line, Beth replied as noncommittally as possible that she and Carla really didn't associate outside of the Canasta group, why? Was there something she should know?

OLD LADY PORN

"Have you ever noticed that Carla doesn't give a tinker's good goddamn about anyone else?" Jenny began. "If you told her that you had to have your foot amputated tomorrow, she'd say how *terribly* sorry she was, but if you, on your crutches, saw her two days later, she wouldn't even ask how you were doing. She's all about her. As long as she thinks that she's coming off as shiny and bright, everyone else is nonexistent."

After a significant draw on her Manhattan, Beth asked if something had happened between Carla and Jenny to have her sputtering so?

After a tirade that required two more rounds of drinks and lots of tears to wind down, the gist of the story was that Jenny's dad was in the end stages of pancreatic cancer. It had been his choice to forego treatment for the already fatal when discovered cancer, but it had been *Carla's* choice to hide the whole ordeal from everyone and to not even allow hospice to come into the picture when the doctor suggested it. After all, how would it *look*? Carla had even kept her husband from sharing the news with his friends and kids. Jenny had only found out because she happened to call her dad when Carla wasn't home; he was drugged out on painkillers and spilled the news. Now she knew why the bitch had been talking about the flu and all those other reasons that no one could get together with dad recently.

Beth was speechless.

It was only two nights later that Jenny's dad was dead. And only ten days before Carla was scheduled to host the rotating monthly Canasta meeting and its annual gift exchange at her house.

Naturally, everyone assumed that the meeting would be re-scheduled and had begun checking their calendars when they received the texts and emails informing them that the party was on as planned.

Six days after burying her husband? Plastic Carla was holding a *party*? Cell phone batteries died in droves.

Finally, it was decided that, if that's what Carla really wanted (and she had been adamant) they should all show up, gifts and all, as awkward as it promised to be.

The Friday of the gift exchange luncheon turned out to be drizzly and gray, but the 'party' mood wasn't dampened by flattened hair and wet shoes, it was dampened by the grim circumstance of the whole thing. Carla had flung open the door wearing a low-cut, high-fashion black cocktail dress, platform shoes and the reddest lipstick any of these women had seen outside of old movies. Things went downhill from there and the whole shebang ended quietly and early.

OLD LADY PORN

When the housekeeper let herself into Carla's house on Monday morning, she was shocked at the party debris that she walked into. The mister had only been dead a week or two and *this*?! And the place stank to high heaven. As usual, the housekeeper began gathering up laundry items as she worked her way toward the utility room.

Already unsettled by the extraordinary condition of the place, the poor woman ran screaming when she discovered Carla's body half in and half out of the washing machine. Dead of course, Carla was firmly anchored by an extravagant scarf wound firmly around both her neck and the agitator. The stench from her release of body fluids and excrement was overpowering and the once sparkly party dress was befouled and limp. To say nothing of the condition of her hair.

Undoubtedly *not* the glamorous, theatrical exit Carla would have orchestrated for herself.

Leslie Baker

A Tidbit

What now, girl! You've been wailing and rending your clothes for days, but you don't tell me what I can do about it.

But... but, you're God. If you don't know how to fix this, who does?

My job isn't to wave a wand and make your life perfect, Marla. My job is to facilitate. If you won't think your problems through enough to help me help you, then I can't do much. Give me something to work with, here.

Lord! My mama's dying, my daughter's taken up with a bum and the roof's leaking. Where the hell do you want me to start?!

I'm in the middle of a poker game; let's talk again when you've gotten ahold of yourself.

What's ... are you inhaling? Smoking?! And poker? In heaven? What the hell kind of place are you running up there?

Oh, girl. What could be better than smoking without stench or cancer? And drinking without hangovers or cirrhosis? Your daddy and the Reeves' are saving your mama's place at the bridge table while every old hound your daddy ever loved is flopped all around him. And ... Dang! Look there! Now your daughter's bum of a grampa-in-law has just taken the pot while I'm lollygagging around with you!

I'll let up on the rain for a day or two, but fixing that roof is on you. Don't be nippin' at me again until you have a good strong chat with yourself. We're in this together, girl, I can't do it all.

OLD LADY PORN

A Halloween Scare

It was Halloween when the elderly sisters arrived in Palm Springs for a few days of sun and fun. That first evening they went to a festival on the streets of downtown, a weekly event featuring hordes of people with (in honor of the holiday) extravagant costumes; some funny, some creative, some cute. Lots of costumed pets accompanied their owners. The girls had a wonderful time.

The next day, after a leisurely breakfast, the two headed to same street to shop and walked smack into a massive gay pride parade. Guys in thong bikinis (with more bare jiggling butt cheeks than one would ever care to see), women so butch the girls got a little nervous and many rainbow couples *way* too demonstrative in their attentions to each other. Most likely these were the costume wearing people from last night's street festival and most of them had looked a hell of a lot better then. After their first amazement began to wear off, the ladies' attention turned back to shopping; it was almost impossible to get from store to store but these were seasoned shoppers and they prevailed.

While it wasn't exactly the Palm Springs they'd envisioned, they were game old gals and after an afternoon of sunning by the pool, indulging in a couple of Margaritas and catching forty winks, they dove back into the fray.

On the agenda for the evening was The Red Room for dinner and a show advertised as a cabaret singer and some comedy. Dinner was delicious and they settled back anticipating equally high-quality entertainment. Well, no. What showed up instead were two of the most vulgar, down and dirty drag queens you could ever find.

This wasn't just funny gay gags. This was vulgar descriptions of positions, entry points and intimate physical features of sex partners. It was more than either of the women could just brush off; truly gross. Use your imagination...it still wouldn't be up to the coarseness. Animals on stage would have had more shame. The audience, who appeared to be 99% gay, thought it was hilarious. It wasn't funny to the only two old, white-haired, cherub faced women trying to smile and shrink into the darkness of the room.

OLD LADY PORN

They were seated in a manner that made it impossible to escape without becoming targets of verbal abuse. They had no choice but to tough it out until intermission when they were finally able to get out and sprint (after a fashion) to the car.

With the doors locked and the windows up, the sisters eventually took a couple of deep breaths before looking at each other and laughing themselves silly over the embarrassment of it all. There would, however, be words spoken later about who had done the research that had landed them in the most notorious gay supper club in town.

Leslie Baker

Eric's Challenge

"Would you mind waiting until we're finished here to do all of that?" the woman seated at a table in the main meeting room of the arts center asked the fellow. "All of *what?*" he belligerently shot back. "Dragging every stick of furniture in here from one end of the room to the other," the old gal replied while trying to keep a smile in her voice.

This was sure poor planning on someone's part, and it wasn't the first time it had happened. The community Arts Center was a building that offered a venue for local artists to meet and display their wares. Whether they painted, sculpted, shared creative writing or played music, there were meetings of all kinds of groups held in this bright, pleasant space.

The only other time anyone could remember such seriously faulty space assignments was several years ago when an evening Wine and Art get-together had been scheduled in the same room where the Saw and Dremel group was holding their monthly demonstration. Luckily, in a case like that, the wine is almost always going to be the persuading factor, so the people with power tools soon packed them up and accepted a glass of bubbly.

On *this* day, when the old lady's request that the elderly guy in the jaunty straw hat quit trying to prepare his concert space at the same time the writer's group was having its readings, things went off the tracks. Suddenly, two fellows who seemed unlikely sparring partners were in a contest and the refined Arts Center, which sure didn't *feel* like an arena for fisticuffs, *was* one.

The bard from the writer's group had abruptly pushed his chair back, grabbed his walker and wobbled across the room to plant himself in front of Straw Hat's current piece of mobile furniture. When Straw Hat began to maneuver the lectern around Bard, the poet deftly shoved one leg of his walker into the open shelf and wrenched the entangled pieces until they crashed to the floor. Straw Hat grabbed Bard by the shoulders and tried to steer him back toward the group's table. Having none of that, Bard pulled a pretty showy move that landed them both on the floor next to the lectern and walker mess while sending the hat rolling under a table.

By then, the other members of Bard's group were trying to intervene without hurting anyone or being taken out themselves. Easier said than done! Bard had grabbed a handful of Straw Hat's newly revealed white hair while Straw Hat was grappling for a hold on Bard's wool vest. Four scrawny old legs were flailing for a hold while visions of broken hips filled the air.

It didn't take long for their early enthusiasm to be overtaken by shortness of breath, leaving Bard and Straw Hat wheezing in the stillness.

One of the three old gals in Bard's group brought a cane over to help pull the combatants up from the floor while the youngest writer got on his knees to steady and support the warriors in their ascent.

No telling who was the first to start giggling, but in the exhilaration of completed battle, it was contagious and soon everyone involved was roaring.

Leslie Baker

OLD LADY PORN

Rosie and the Boys

The sun was just over the roof of the single-story apartment complex as Rosie sashayed into the pool area. A customary cigarette dangled from her bottom lip as she juggled a large beach bag, ratty beach towel and coffee mug.

Not that there was a *beach* anywhere for miles, but Palm Desert is beach weather all year if you love the heat. Rosie clearly fell into that category with her leathery, wrinkled skin the color of a hazelnut and sun-frazzled, sometimes gray/sometimes blond hair. She never wore a cover-up over the saggy swimsuit encasing her barrel belly over spindly legs.

As she made her way to her 'morning chair' a couple of other loungers offered greetings in the quiet camaraderie of regulars. During the cooler months, the winter visitors had to be unceremoniously indoctrinated in the courtesy shown to year-round residents: their 'chairs' were *theirs* and not to be appropriated by newbies; music on portable radios was subject to group approval; no snitching to the manager if alcohol was detected and Rosie Rules. Period.

There were a few actual chairs around umbrellaed tables scattered here and there, but the regulars referred to their preferred chaise lounges as chairs and you were expected to pick up on this quickly. Rosie had a morning and an afternoon chair so she could maintain her tan in optimal condition.

Some days, Rosie was taciturn and others she was gregarious and chatty; it was best to see which before initiating any conversation with her. It was hard to say where she was from, her accent said The Bronx to someone who'd never been out of the desert southwest. Like many elderly women who had been lookers in their youth, Rosie forgot what she had seen as soon as she looked away from the morning mirror; she was still the beautiful, young Rosie. Unless everything hurt, then she snarled her way through the day. If the thermos of vodka in her bag had begun to flow, the Rosie of the Day was enhanced.

The men in Rosie's life put in only sporadic appearances at the pool and rarely together. The two of them, Bald and Balder, were supposedly Rosie's husband and his brother. Both of the boys were rotund and unfriendly to each other, Rosie and everyone else. The three of them shared an apartment and a huge old Cadillac with a battered convertible top.

Some version of these three could likely be seen in every apartment compound in every sun belt town. Even their sad downfall probably isn't unique.

That hot summer day, there were only a couple of the regulars, including Rosie, braving the sizzling pool area when four or five black cars snaked through the parking lot and disappeared from sight further into the sprawling property. Rosie, saying nothing, teetered up from her chaise and left at some speed, leaving all of her things behind.

None of those beach things or the ransacked possessions littering their apartment were ever claimed by Rosie, Bald or Balder. A couple of neighbors had seen the three being unceremoniously escorted into the black cars with their hands cuffed behind their backs and spirited off, but other than the slamming of doors and drawers inside the apartment, no one had heard anything that could tell the rest of the story.

Leslie Baker

Yesterday's News
Old Trees and Old Women

I've spent most of my life disliking juniper trees. For one thing, they tend to be grayish rather than a bright, true green and many varieties are messy and ratty looking.

Then, about fifteen years ago, we bought a lot to build a spec house on. The lot had been semi-cleared by a previous owner and we did the bare minimum more clearing in order to accommodate the footprint of the house. The market crashed around then and we ended up living in that house for a couple of years. While doing the landscaping, we were confronted with several junipers which had been partially dozed over and mostly uprooted years earlier but were still alive.

Those unique trees became the highlights of our beautiful backyard. You'd have to have a harder heart than I to not appreciate the resiliency and determination shown by those trees. Where we live now is a botanist's encyclopedia of Juniper varieties. You name it and I imagine it's here somewhere. Ron Kemble has patiently pointed out the distinctions to me over the years, but I don't retain them very well. I may not be sure of all their names, but I love those quirky trees. They are tough as nails and ain't goin' down without a fight!

Junipers are kind of like me and the fight I'm putting up over going gracefully gray.

Last week as I set out to run a few errands, I was appalled at the state of my hair. When the shopping was finished, I swung by my hairdresser's place to see if she might be able to squeeze me in for a haircut. Katie only sees me once or twice a year and by the time I throw myself on her mercy, she has to bite her tongue to not ask what brand of weed-eater I've been using to cut my own hair.

I was whisked through a cut and a primer on how to go gray with the least amount of fuss. I had asked because the time is here when I'm going to have to do it and it's a bitter decision to be facing. I'm already old, but gray? *Really?* This old age crap just gets better and better.

The most fun part of an hour in a hairstylist's chair is the chance to solve all of the world's problems. I admire how an experienced stylist can carry on conversations with people of differing viewpoints, maintain her sunny attitude and not stab those scissors into the carotid artery

OLD LADY PORN

of some of the more opinionated clients. There's a reason I never took up barbering.

Whether we're talking old trees or old women, we're a tough bunch and, when the fight is over, life may have knocked us down, turned us gray and broken a few limbs, but we fought the good fight. We will go to our reward with no whimpering and proud of the life we lived.

Leslie Baker

Old Lady Porn

The two nicely dressed old ladies were having lunch in a local spot when one of them literally screamed with laughter, eliciting a few looks over raised forks.

"How did you *know?!*" yelped Karen when she could finally speak again.

"What? Know you had a vibrator stashed away and that, if you're actually *dying*, you might want to dispose of it before the kids start cleaning out your house?" Luanne asked in return.

This of course, began a conversation that went in a wholly different direction than the somber one the ladies had begun when their coffees were delivered.

Yes folks, women of all ages have ongoing relationships with their vibrators. And the older a woman gets, the more likely it is that Buddy is her only steady sex partner. So it *shouldn't* shock the kids when they run across these things among Mom's possessions, but children tend to see their parents (and mothers in particular) as asexual beings concerned only with volunteer work and grandchildren.

Ah, you innocent little sweets, where do you think *you* came from? At some point most young kids have to face the fact the stork didn't deliver them to their parents' doorstep; but it's still the default image they prefer to contemplating other options. Which works until the "Aaaarrrgh!!" moment when their 90-year-old mother has breathed her last, the house has to be readied for market, and there, tucked away conveniently close to the bed is the evidentiary tool. Yowza.

A few years ago, I began noticing an ever-growing selection of old-lady-porn showing up in the middle of catalogs peddling gingham cafe-curtains and old-fashioned potato mashers. I've never understood how I get on all of these mailing lists for catalogs offering stuff which is completely off base from what I actually buy. But florescent pink dildos with many and varied textures, sizes and appendages? Right next to hot pads with peaches on them? That gives you a pretty good idea of who the intended market for 'personal massagers' is. Can you imagine the sort of catalogs flooding your mailbox if you ever actually *ordered* one of those sex toys out of The Cozy Country Catalog?

OLD LADY PORN

A lot of us might think the mortification of receiving such a catalog (or some of the goods therein) would be worth it if that hunky delivery driver came with the package. If he harbored secret cravings for saggy, wrinkled old bags his grandmother's age. Oh, baby! Lock the door and turn out the lights. Who's never eyed the high, tight rear end of the young fellow mixing a gallon of paint and thought there were better uses for that waist-high vibrating paint mixer? Or thought a waiter's thighs were totally wasted in delivering a round of beers when the barstool could provide other options?

Old women may not dish any details, but they might be comforted to realize that they're part of a large sisterhood who are old in body but not in spirit!

Leslie Baker

Hope You Enjoyed *Old Lady Porn*

I'd be so appreciative if you would review the book on Amazon, Goodreads or wherever you buy and discuss your books. While there's nothing as delightful as a *good* review, there's nothing as helpful as an *honest* review, so don't spare my feelings!

If you haven't yet read my first book, *Fireworks!* it's still on Amazon. In spite of its 'first book' glitches, it remains a pertinent read for boomers and their children.

I'm on Facebook and would love to hear from you.

Leslie Baker

Fireworks!

Have you ever wondered about your parents or your adult children:

'What on God's great green earth are they *thinking?!*' Boomers and their Millennial children grew up in different Americas and are now trying to understand each other and their quickly evolving world.

MeToo, Guns, Geriatric sex, Male (and female!) Toxicity, Hospice, Politics and Gender neutrality...what's not to like?
It's a short read and will have you cussing in no time!

Fireworks! is a profane, irreverent and political look at the Baby Boomers in old age and at the Millennials they raised. Not for the faint of heart.

Printed in the USA
CPSIA information can be obtained
at www.ICGtesting.com
LVHW010614150524
780342LV00001B/163